It was my usual practice during my first day back after a long trip, to retire early. And so it was that that night after dinner and a few drinks, I bade Cora goodnight and climbed the stairs. I opened the bedroom door and snapped on the lights to reveal the little present Cora had prepared for me.

Nichole lay stretched out on her back on the silken sheets of my bed. She was totally naked except for leather straps at her throat, wrists, and ankles. From these she had been spread-eagled, her limbs tied to convenient posts at the corners of the bed. Her long body was tense with the strain as arms, legs, and thighs were pulled taut by the leather strips. She was also blindfolded. I don't know how long she had been waiting for me there in that darkened room.

IRONWOOD
Revisited

DON WINSLOW

BLUE MOON BOOKS, INC. NEW YORK

Published by Blue Moon Books, Inc.
841 Broadway, Fourth Floor
New York, NY 10003

Ironwood Revisited
ISBN 1-56201-060-3
CIP data available from the Library of Congress

Manufactured in the United States of America

FOREWORD

The Ironwood papers only recently came to light, after being discovered in an abandoned house in Copenhagen. The story they tell is exotic, sometimes bizarre, and largely unbelievable. And yet rumors of such a place as Ironwood, so meticulously described in those pages, continue to persist.

The early papers describe how the writer, known to us only as "James," became involved with a unique enterprise called "Ironwood." In IRONWOOD REVISITED his saga continues, as the reader is invited to return to that legendary training institution. In this volume, edited from the later papers in the Ironwood documents, we once again follow the account of James, the lascivious entrepreneur, who has risen to the top in his most unusual business organization.

A few years older than when last we met, James has gradually developed the strength of character, maturity, and discriminating taste that marks him as a man of the world. In the process he encounters the beautiful, the rich and the powerful, all sharing his obsession with sexual experiences. From them he learns of new horizons to explore as he is introduced into the most exquisite realms of sensual pleasure.

His journey is marked by a gradual appreciation of the meaning of the training which Ironwood imposes on its young charges. He learns that what dominates it all is something undefinable, something that can only be experienced as the spirit of Ironwood.

Don Winslow
Copenhagen, Denmark

CHAPTER ONE

A Homecoming of Sorts

It had been five years since I had first stood before Cora Blasingdale seated at her massive desk in the office at Ironwood. Now our positions were reversed as I sat behind that desk, and she stood in front waiting for me to give her permission to sit down. I let her wait.

Five years made this an anniversary of sorts. They had been good years and Ironwood had prospered. Our business, supplying well-trained young ladies to various houses of pleasure and private collectors throughout the world, was flourishing. Ironwood had acquired a reputation, albeit among a very small and select group of connoisseurs, of offering, for a very pretty price, the finest quality and most thoroughly trained sex slaves in the world.

It was my principle assistant, Cora Blasingdale, who was responsible for maintaining the strict standards and iron discipline that in-

fused our training, making it world famous.
For once a young woman graduated from
Ironwood, she had only one purpose left in
life—to serve without reservation, to place her
body and her mind in the sexual service of
her master. She no longer had a will of her
own, her single remaining desire was to please.
To that end she sought to be used or abused
by a master who would totally dominate her.
Her happiness lay in giving herself completely,
in abject submission to the will of the other.

For this spirit of Ironwood, Cora was largely
responsible. Standing before me now, in her
all-black outfit, tight turtleneck sweater, jodhpurs, and riding boots, I was reminded of
that fateful day when I had forced her to
strip in front of the Ironwood community,
subjugating her, bending her to my will.

She seemed to bear little resentment over
that incident, the public humiliation she had
been forced to endure. I couldn't help notic-
ing that when she spoke now the hard edge
was no longer in her voice. Rather, her words
were soft, caressing, with a hint of tender-
ness. She spoke in the voice of a humble
lover. But I ignored her pleading tone; my
responses curt, business-like. I kept the tall
blond standing before me making her give a
detailed report of the happenings at Ironwood during my absence. When she was done,
she added, plaintively, that she had missed
me. I looked at her face, and saw that her
eyes had softened in sexual desire.

"You may sit down," I said gesturing to the

chair in front of me. "And take off your boots, and the pants," I added, making it sound like an afterthought, a casual, offhanded remark.

Without a word, she seated herself facing me and obediently bent over to struggle with the long tight boots. Then her hands went to the waistband of her riding pants and she worked those over her hips down the firm contours of her thighs and legs, and off her feet. She had put on black pantyhose under her jodhpurs and, in accordance with my standing instructions, no panties. The thick blond tuft of her triangle was clearly visible plastered against the sheer nylon. She sat with her back straight in the chair, her knees apart, presenting me with a lewd display showing the pale shadow of her pussy spread between her nyloned thighs.

I studied the proud blond her lower body encased in the smoky haze of black nylon as she posed there, perfectly still: shoulders back, chin high, eyes hard and bright with growing excitement. I lit a cigarette, and after contemplating her wanton form for several minutes I whispered my orders to her:

"Now the sweater and bra."

She wrestled with the snug sweater pulling it up over her head. Then, with her eyes locked on mine, she reached behind her to unloosen the black frilly brassiere, letting the lacy straps fall forward down her arms with a shrug, revealing a pair of wide based globes set low on her torso. Released from their confines they showed just the slightest sag with soft pink aureoles, two wide disks capping the lovely swells.

I decided to have some fun with her.

"You know you have such pretty tits. I want to see you play with them. Go on, show me how you do it."

Without hesitation she leaned back and brought her hands to her breasts, cupping herself. She grinned wickedly as she closed her fingers over the globes and squeezed. Then she began to massage the soft handfuls of flesh with a slow circular motion. Her eyelids fluttered closed and she rolled her head, sunk in blissful rapture as she dreamily caressed herself.

"Get those nipples hard. Work on them!" I snapped.

She looked down through half-lidded eyes and her hands stopped their movements. With delicate precision, she pinched the tips between thumbs and fingers and squeezed, forcing the little stems to protrude. Then she plucked at her nipples, gently pulling on them, stretching the pliant flesh. Her swollen nipples stiffened in reaction, pointing slightly up and out, hard and erect, taut with excitement.

"Those nipples look good enough to suck. Go on, try it. I'll bet they're big enough for you to be able to get to them. Show me!" I commanded.

Cora obeyed me instantly. She reached down and cupping her right boob squeezed the shape to elongate it so she could force the tip towards her straining mouth. Her long thin tongue flickered out to lightly touch the darkening tip. Then she was licking it up and down. Bending still further, she shoved the tip into her mouth and began sucking on it. The sensuous sight of this passionate blond hollowing her cheeks as she sucked her own tit, just about drove me crazy. I was so stiff it ached, and I reached down behind the desk to loosen my pants releasing my swollen throbbing cock. Cora was now totally engrossed in her task.

"Enough," I managed to get out.

She released her breast and I watched the wet mound ploop out, the glistening tip hard and proudly erect. Things were getting out of hand and I knew I would either have to lay into this woman, or risk shooting my wad all over my pants.

"Get over to the desk. Belly up to the front, and lean over it." My voice sounded hoarse, and my throat was dry.

I kicked off my shoes along with my pants and skimmed my briefs down my legs. Then, wearing only my white silk shirt, I strode around the front of the desk to stand behind the bending form. Her breasts hung heavily under her. I placed a hand on the small of her back forcing her down onto the desk, crushing her globes under her, and caressing the lovely swells of her upturned bottom. Then I pushed my straining cock up against the rounded hillocks still encased in smoky nylon. I rubbed the shaft against the silky smooth-

ness up and down the darker shadowline between the rubbery slopes.

Impatient now, I grabbed at the waistband
of the pantyhose, and roughly yanked them
down over the swelling mounds and all the
way down her long legs and off her feet,
lifting one foot after the other till she was
free of the nylon. I had her spread her legs
while I ran my hands up their length, savoring those feminine contours. Then I slipped
one hand up between her thighs to cup the
soft pouch of her pussy. She shifted impatiently, widening her legs and giving me
greater access to her steamy cunt. She squatted slightly, pressing her sex against my palm,
rubbing the soft slick folds of her pussylips
against my hand, and moaning softly.

I stepped against her upturned ass and carefully inserted my cock into her slick, dripping
cunt, pushing it home and causing her to jerk
and grunt in reaction. Then she was squirming back to meet my push, shoving her swelling mounds back against my thrusting hips,
seeking to bury me deeper in her hot core.
My hands tightened around her hips as I
rode her to the ragged edge of passion. With
a violent tremor she came, shaking and crying
out in a long, plaintive "Ooooh." My own climax quickly followed as with a deep gut-
wrenching shudder, I exploded sending a
pulsating jet of sperm up her cunt before I
sagged weakly and collapsed on top of the
still bent-over female.

We rested gasping for breath and panting

heavily as the waves of passion subsided. Wearily I climbed off of her and fell back into a waiting chair. She let herself slide off the desk to the floor and crawled over between my sprawled legs to sit back, resting her head against my inner thigh. She smiled up at me and whispered.

"Welcome home, Master James."

*   *   *

I traveled often now on various business affairs, and my intervals at Ironwood were brief and far between. Cora resolved to see that my precious time there was pleasantly spent. She became attentive and solicitous about my comfort. As a gesture of her concern, Cora saw to it that for each night I spent at Ironwood I would have suitable companionship. On occasion I would specify who I wanted and what arrangements should be made. But often I left it up to Cora's fertile imagination to choose from among the lovely residents those who might interest me, to dress them properly, and to instruct them carefully with my pleasure in mind.

Tonight Nichole had been selected as the one to be placed at my disposal for the evening. She was a dark-eyed slender woman of nineteen, with sharp features and a slightly oriental look to her small face. That look was enhanced by straight jet-black hair worn in bangs across her forehead and falling to her shoulders in a single silken sheath behind. Of all the females I had known at Ironwood, Nichole was the most sensual. Even without

the Ironwood training with its unrelenting
focus on her sexuality to constantly stimulate
her, she would have been a totally sexual
being. She had a lively interest in all things
erotic, and her enthusiasm was infectious.

It was my usual practice during my first
day back after a long trip, to retire early. And
so it was that that night after dinner and a
few drinks, I bade Cora goodnight and climbed
the stairs. I opened the bedroom door and
snapped on the lights to reveal the little present Cora had prepared for me.

Nichole lay stretched out on her back on
the silken sheets of my bed. She was totally
naked except for leather straps at her throat,
wrists, and ankles. From these she had been
spread-eagled, her limbs tied to convenient
posts at the corners of the bed. Her long
body was tense with the strain as arms, legs,
and thighs were pulled taut by the leather
strips. She was also blindfolded. I don't know
how long she had been waiting for me there
in that darkened room.

I decided to let her wait awhile longer. I
leisurely strode to bathroom, then slowly
stripped and wrapped my nakedness in a short
silk kimono.

Then, very quietly, I crept close to the unsuspecting female stretched out on my bed. I
stood beside her scarcely breathing, as I gazed
down on the taut body. Her hair, tucked in
by the blindfold strap, was fanned out on the
silk between her long thin white arms. Her
slender torso, stretched taut, showed a slight

depression at her belly, narrow hips with prominent hip bones, trim thighs, and sleek long haunches. Her legs were long and rather straight, sleek and slightly curved, the lines flowed to delicate ankles and feet.

I studied her proud breasts, two pert cones perched high on her chest and slightly flattened by her position. They were tipped with two tiny, perfectly-formed nipples nestled in quiet repose in the soft brown crinkled flesh of her aureoles. My eyes swept over the maidenly breasts and down the hollow of her belly to the prominent little mound at its base sprinkled with tiny coils of black pussyhair. The dark centerfold and the fleshy cuntlips lay exposed by the angle of her spread legs.

I reached out to lightly brush the pads of two fingertips across her left nipple. She stifled a cry at the unexpected touch, flinching reflexively and jerking on her bounds, sending her tits jiggling. I pulled my hand away and waited. The room was perfectly silent and still except for the slight movement of her breasts as they gently rose and fell with her even breathing. She parted her lips and let out a long sigh.

Next I placed my fingertips in the palm of her hand, weaving little circles on that soft flesh. Her hand trembled slightly in confused response. She clenched her small fist capturing my teasing fingers. Patiently I waited till she opened her hand, then traced across her palm and down over the wide strap banding the wrist. Then, following a delicate blue vein,

my touch glided down the smooth flesh of
her inner arm to caress her shoulder and
pass on to the moist softness of her exposed
armpit, with its faint black stubble.

For a few seconds I teased her in that most
sensitive area. Her hips bounced and her fists
clenched. I decided to spare her the sweet
torment of my friendly tickling, and moved
my hand down her side along the delicate
ribcage, resting it for a moment on her hip.

Her breathing was heavier now. My teasing
fingers were beginning to get to her. I traced
a line from hipbone to hipbone, across her
flat belly, and upward into a slight hollow,
then on to her chest up the narrow path
between her firm little breasts. Placing three
fingers under her left tit I bounced it lightly,
flopping it up and down. Then, reasoning
that two hands were better than one when
two handfuls were available, I brought my
left hand up to capture her other boob. Now
I played with her breasts, sliding my hands
over the soft masses, kneading the pretty
shapes, testing their resiliency, squeezing the
spongy softness.

After a few minutes of this her nipples
responded, the tiny stems emerging from their
dormant state. I looked up at her face. Her
lips were parted; her breathing ragged. She
began tossing her head from side to side, my
intense manipulations heating her up while
all the while she was emitting urgent whim-
pers of desire. I pulled back to watch. Her
tongue peeked out to quickly rim her lips. I

waited till her heaving chest began to subside a little, then I started in again.

Now I clamped my hands deliberately on those satiny globes and closed them, firmly capturing her tits in my warm grasp. As I clenched my hands I watched the soft flesh bulge between my closing fingers. My black-haired beauty let out a long moan of passion and thrust her chest up to meet me, driving her tits with their small, hard nipples, into my palms.

She gave out a series of "ohs," each rising in intensity. Finally she shrieked as a little spasm shook her taut body. Then she was still. Gasping and panting for air, her tortured breasts heaving in great swells.

Letting her rest for awhile, I calmly walked across the room to fix myself a drink. At Ironwood each bedroom contained a well-stocked bar. I dumped some ice in a large glass, poured a generous helping of scotch, splashed in a little water, and sat down to wait, contemplating my next move.

I left a quarter hour lapse in silence. Then I walked to the foot of the bed to study the outstretched naked form. An inspired idea came to me. Digging an ice cube out of my glass, I reached down towards the unsuspecting female. She shrieked and jerked on her straps as I applied the frozen cube to the bottom pad of a dainty little foot.

Since she had difficulty controlling her reaction, I clasped her foot with my other hand, and holding her steady, began to tickle her toes with the dripping cube, watching them curl in reaction. Then I glided the wet cube onto the top of her foot, over the ankle strap, and up along a tightly-muscled calve. A glistening trail of moisture traced my path up the long graceful curve of her leg and across to the smooth silky flesh on the inside of her straining thigh.

Now she was churning in a frenzy of activity, twisting, wriggling, and squirming under the relentless advance of the little cube. I thoroughly rubbed it over every inch of her inner thighs, coating them with a thin sheen of water. I couldn't resist leaning over her and touching the tip of my tongue to the wet soft flesh. Licking up and down over the smooth surface, I felt her shiver in delight.

I reached back into the glass, grabbing two cubes this time, and smacking them tight against the love pouch at the center of her underarch. She whooped in surprise at the sudden cold shock. I let her heat melt them a little, pressed as they were against the soft folds of warm flesh, then I grasped them between thumb and finger and traced the outline of her pussy lips.

She let out a single tiny moan, like a hurt animal. With my other hand I opened her up and slid the cubes just into the glistening silky channel, poking them into place with a single finger. She responded with an abrupt "ugh," as I shoved the cubes all the way up her twat. Her little moans of urgency turned into a long quivering "oooh," as she shuddered once, twice, then once again.

"Oh, take it out it's so cold. Please. Oh, oh, oh," she whimpered.

I ignored her, preferring to wait till the inner warmth melted the frozen lumps deep in her core. She lay there moaning softly, occasionally tossing her head, thrashing the bed with her silken hair, her hips slowly squirming on the silk as the exciting tingle radiated out from her cunt.

Since the cold stimulation up her twat had obviously excited her I looked around for ways to increase her pleasure, and keep our little game going.

I remembered that the bar was equipped with a small refrigerator, and that two bottles of champagne were always kept on ice. I went to retrieve one. Popping the cork, I took a long deep draft, then I shook the bottle lightly, holding my thumb over the top. Bottle in hand, I advanced on my blindfolded victim, determined to provide her with a unique erotic sensation, her first champagne douche.

With one quick motion I removed my thumb and plunged the neck of the bottle into her cunt, a spray of lively foam drenching her stomach, tits, and crotch, along with my silk robe. She shrieked and whooped and hollared as the bubbling froth scoured her insides. I shoved the icy bottle deeper, lodging it firmly between her bouncing thighs. It bobbed obscenely between her legs as her hips bucked and thrashed in wild excitement.

My own excitement was now rising to a
fever pitch as I bent to free her ankles allowing her to flail her legs, scissoring them spasmodically, squeezing the sturdy bottle between
her powerful thighs. Next I unclipped her
wrist straps, leaving the blindfold in place.
Her freed hands went immediately to the bottle, but I stopped her with a sharp command,
reminding her that I had shoved it up her
there and she would wear it until I pulled it
out. At that she squirmed and rolled onto her
side, wriggling and hunching over the bottle,
working her hips, fucking herself on the cold
hard neck penetrating her core.

I decided the time was ripe to replace this
glass dildo with the real thing. I grabbed her
roughly by the hips and turned her over onto
her back. Clasping the base of the bottle, I
diddled her with it a few times before yanking it out. It popped free of her dripping
cunt with a slurping sound, the neck gleaming with her love juices mixed with a generous dose of bubbly foam.

I scrambled onto the bed and plunged into
her thorougly soaked cunt. A numbing, tinglng
coldness greeted me as I slipped my prick
along the silken walls of her inner channel.
The tingling excitement drove me deeper into
her, our movements making tiny squishy
sounds. I looked down to see my shaft emerge
from her wet sucking lips covered with tiny
bubbles. The bucking girl flung her arms and
legs around me, her thighs gripping my hips,
urging me on, thumping my butt with her

heels and meeting each plunge with her own demanding thrust.

Now she was babbling incoherently, delerious in wild abandon. A series of convulsive contractions racked her thin frame, sending me over the edge at the same time. I came with a violent tremor, crushing my groin against her sopping hole, flooding her belly with my sperm in a long series of powerful thrusts.

*   *   *

Basking in the afterglow, we sprawled on the bed, propped up on pillows, sharing a cigarette. My arm was around her shoulders and I idly toyed with a tit as we talked. The blindfold had been removed, and Nichole snuggled against me, her head in the hollow of my shoulder, her silken hair lightly teasing my chest.

She told me how the sudden stab of the chilled bottle had thrilled her to the core, the shock of that penetrating, painfully-cold shaft sending spasms of pulsating pleasure rocketing through her body. As she talked, I began to devise a little experiment.

Leaving her propped up on the bed, a drink in one hand, I padded over to the bathroom to rummage through the medicine chest. Finding the pack of prophylactics I was hunting for, I extracted one of the thin rubber membranes, filling it with water at the sink. Then I opened the freezer compartment of the bar's refrigerator and carefully suspended the sausage-shaped balloon from a rack inside. If I was right, my experiment would take several hours to freeze, and it should be solid by morning. I closed the freezer door, and went back to join my naked companion on the bed, grabbing the remaining champagne bottle on the way.

Nichole seemed to have recovered from her blind frenzied ordeal. She was chatting on about the feel of bubbly champagne on one's most intimate parts, like a thousand tiny finger tips teasing the sensitive flesh. She meekly asked if I'd like to try it, and seemed delighted when I gave my assent.

She poured a little of the foamy liquid into her palm and dumped it onto my crotch, the sudden cold caused me to flinch. Then she gently rubbed it into the springy pubic hairs, along my cock, and down into the hairy sack of my balls. She did this several times, thoroughly soaking my masculine equipment in champagne. I tingled with a slight burning sensation. Then she dove on me, taking my semi-hard prick into the hot, wet cavern of her little mouth.

Her moist lips circled my shaft and traveled down the entire length. I clenched my fists in an effort to maintain control. Then she pulled out the saliva-coated tool, and gripping it more firmly at the base, extended her tongue to the sensitive tip, flicking at it, slithering around the knob, laving and teasing the firm swollen hardon from the crown to base. Then her lips were on my balls, gently taking them into her mouth and licking the tingling bubbles caught in the hairs on the sack. I opened my legs wider as her probing tongue rooted deep under my crotch.

Then she shifted, a sexy grin on her face, pleased to be giving pleasure. Kneeling beside me, she reached down to wrap her delicate fingers around my swollen shaft, bending my straining prick towards her hot wet mouth. She captured the crown and slid her mouth down the shaft, hollowing her cheeks in a slow suck. I reached down to grab a handful of silky black hair on her bobbing head, hoping to hold on as long as I could.

But I couldn't withstand the sweet torment of that slithering tongue, and, my control slipping away, I was sent rocketing into space, pumping a geyser of sperm into her talented little mouth. She swallowed it all, smacking her lips and humming in satisfaction. Then she worked on thoroughly cleaning the residue from my tender, depleted cock.

I soon realized that sexy little Nichole was just as inventive as I in the games of love. After a few minutes rest, she had me turn over onto my stomach.

Next she grabbed the bottle, pouring a stream of the lively liquid onto my back, letting it trickle down into the crack between my butt. I clenched my cheeks at the sudden cold splash and jerked my ass in response, but she placed a gentle hand on the small of my back to steady me, and poured a little more into the dark valley.

Now I felt the faint tickle of long silky hair sweeping across the backs of my thighs. Suddenly her lively tongue was in my crack, licking and sucking up the runny liquid. She slowly trailed up and down between my cheeks, making little slurping noises, the wet softness sending jolts of pleasure through my body. Incredibly, I felt my cock begin to stir. Then she was concentrating her attention on my asshole, stabbing at that little target with her straining tongue. I groaned as a wave of ecstatic delight swept over me.

With a deep sigh I rolled over, reaching out to her and pulling her close to stop the sweet torture. I kissed her long and hard, her lips, mouth, and chin glistening wet with champagne. And I whispered a goodnight. Totally drained of passion, I sank into blissful sleep, my little bedmate snuggled beside me. The last words I remember drifting through my mind were Cora's: "Welcome home, Master James."

*   *   *

The light sneaking around the heavy drapes told me it must be morning. I turned to look at the sleeping nude sprawled on her side in gentle repose, her little rounded ass jutting back towards me in lewd invitation. She still wore her ankle and wrist bands; they would come in handy.

I crept quietly out of bed and tiptoed to the freezer to check on my little experiment of the night before. The cock-shaped icicle was frozen solid.

Back at the bed I turned my sleeping companion over onto her stomach. She sighed.

Then I spread her arms to clip her wrists to the short straps still in place at the top corners of the bed. She woke with a start, twisting around to look up at me quizzically. Being a well-trained resident of Ironwood, she knew better than to protest or question what was happening to her. She simply waited patiently to see what was to be done. Nevertheless, I sought to calm her by leaning to whisper in her ear that I had a surprise for her.

I slid down to the foot of the bed to affix her ankles, completing the job by piling two pillows under her stomach, displaying her ass prominently. There were just a few more details to attend to.

I knew from our little escapade of the previous night that she would be far from quiet when I delivered her "present," so I decided to gag her so as not to wake the whole second floor. Fortunately, each guestroom at Ironwood was equipped with various restraining devices, including gags and blindfolds. I selected a thick leather strap which had been passed through a hard rubber ball, about the size of a tennis ball. Submissively, she opened her mouth to receive the ball between her teeth. I cinched the strap across the back of her head, imprisoning the soft black silk. Then, since I wanted the surprise to be complete, I decided to re-apply the blindfold, tying the strip behind her head just above the other band.

Now, satisfied that she had been properly prepared, I went to retrieve her frozen sur-

prise. A few minutes passed as I let her wait
to get adjusted to the darkness and the restraints. Then with the frozen icy shaft in
hand, I studied her spread legs and the easy
access her position provided to the under-
slung pouch of her cunt. I peeled the rubber
sheath up and off the icicle, and slowly moved
to within an inch of my target.

With a single vicious shove I rammed the
cold shaft straight up into her unsuspecting
twat. A muffled scream came from the tethered female who jerked violently on all four
straps, at the sudden penetrating shock. Her
thighs were vibrating and her butt muscles
clamping spasmodically as she squirmed on
the bed, trying desperately to escape the stinging cold of the frozen shaft lodged in her
core. Tiny sounds of urgency escaped from
behind the gag as I twisted the icy rod, screwing her, and shoving it in all the way, burying
it deep within her shivering sex.

Now she was wildly shaking her ass as if
trying to dislodge the little visitor. I toyed
with the dripping end, a little mound of melting ice peeking out obscenely from between
her pussy lips.

Then I climbed on the bed and, sitting on
one of her thrashing legs, I captured the other,
immobilizing it by leaning on it as I unclipped
her ankle straps. Next I roughly pulled her
ankles together locking the frozen shaft deep
between her taut thighs. I wrapped a strap
around both ankles, binding them together,
as Nichole kept up a constant stream of keen-

ing noises. A second strap was applied just below her knees, and a third cinched tightly into place across the top of her straining thighs, running just below the jutting mounds of her tight little ass. Now with her legs tightly bound together, I was sure that the freezing shaft would stay lodged firmly in place, despite her wildest gyrations. It would stay nestled in there until melted by the heat of her inner recesses.

I left her in the darkened room; immobilized, straining against the tight strictures, ass upturned, blindfolded, gagged, and twitching and moaning in pleasure/pain.

I backed out slowly into the hallway, closing the door behind me. The smell of coffee was in the air. And I was suddenly very hungry.

CHAPTER TWO

Of Trials and Tribulations

It being a weekday classes were in full session by the time I finished my leisurely breakfast. I sauntered down the hallway between the classrooms, pausing here and there to watch the eager students, their up-turned, well-scrubbed young faces listening intently to detailed instruction in all facets of human sexual experience. Recently there had been a crop of new arrivals, and the instructors had their hands full.

My meanderings finally took me to the large demonstration room at the far end of the hallway. Here Monique Van Daam, one of Cora's assistants, was conducting a class on deportment. The purpose was to instill, by rigid discipline, a self control so powerful that a girl's calm, feminine poise might be maintained through any trials her master might force her to endure.

I slipped into the back of the classroom. A

group of young pupils were sitting on the floor in a semicircle, their backs to me. They were not aware of my entrance. Not wishing to disrupt the lesson, I quietly sat down behind them to watch the demonstration in progress.

The girl chosen was a leggy, slim-hipped adolescent of about sixteen, who, with her straight blond hair pulled back in a pony tail, looked even younger. She wore the abbreviated pleated skirt and thin white cotton knee socks that were part of the Ironwood schoolgirl's uniform. Her serviceable school shoes had been replaced by a pair of narrow pumps with four inch high stiletto heels. The effect was slightly incongruous, but I soon found that there was a purpose for it. From the waist up she was naked; having discarded her brassiere, blouse, and blazer jacket, at the stern command of her mistress.

Her little adolescent titties were nestled together high on her slender chest. The topless condition was so that her instructor and classmates could closely observe the movements of her breasts. The exercise was to have her walk back and forth across the front of the room with a minimum of sway and bounce to her boobs. To assist in making even the slightest movement plainly noticeable, two little cones had been made out of construction paper, and these had been taped to each nipple, jutting out two inches in front. In order to make the test more interesting, her ankles had been shackled with a short length of light chain, running between two wide leather anklestraps.

Wobbling precariously on her high heels, the effect was to throw her weight forward, tensing the muscles of her taut calves, while she threw back her shoulders and arched her back in an effort to compensate. Maintaining this erect posture, her proud breasts thrust high and the nipples, with their weird extensions, pointing up and outward, she was ordered to begin her walk. But the best she could manage was a series of short, shuffling steps. Our eyes were drawn to the wobbling tits, the paper cones bobbing and weaving with each tiny step.

Her first tentative steps met with the harsh disapproval of Mademosielle Van Daam, who accused her of not trying hard enough. She shouted at the flustered girl to concentrate.

But the hapless creature's next few steps were no better, the telltale cones weaving and jiggling wildly. At that her mistress flicked the riding crop she carried in her right hand towards the girl's behind. We heard a swish as the whippy rod cut the air, and a solid thunk as it landed square on the target. The girl jumped and yelped at the flash of pain, her hands flying behind her to rub away the sting.

Deciding that the wool skirt offered too much protection, Monique ordered her to take it off. Her hands went to the convenient clasp at the side and, with a tug over her hips, the little skirt fell down her narrow legs. She stepped out of it, left with only the thin nylon panties between her vulnerable ass and the stinging whip. She stood at attention in her plain white schoolgirl's panties, kneesocks, high heels, and anklestraps, with the little white cones sticking out obscenely in front of her. The effect was strangely erotic.

Now the lesson began again, as the girl struggled to hold the little cones even. She screwed up her face in intense concentration, taking a few cautious, mincing steps. The whip lashed out again, cutting across her pantied cheeks, causing her to recoil and grasp her stinging behind. And so the lesson proceeded, a few tentative steps, punctuated by a smack on the behind, until Mademoiselle seemed satisfied, and the girl was allowed to, very gingerly, resume her seat on the hard wood floor. I confess that I saw little progress made, but then very often the effort is more important than the results.

For the next demonstration, Mademoiselle had planned on capitalizing on the girls' natural competitiveness by staging a little contest. Three contestants were selected, the object being to see who could maintain her control the longest under similar trying conditions. By way of preparation, the contestants were called to the front of the room and ordered to remove their skirts. Immediately the three little pieces of cloth dropped around their ankles, and they stepped daintily out of them. The blazer jackets were next; then their shoes. When they were ready the girls were lined

up, side by side, facing us. The bottoms of
their short white blouses barely covered their
hips, exposing their thin girlish thighs from
the elastic leg bands of their panties down to
the ribbed tops of the thin cotton socks start-
ing just below their knees.

They were ordered to turn around, their
backs to us, and march to a set of long wooden
bars at the far end of the room. The first of
these was mounted between two saw-horses,
padded, and set waist high for a schoolgirl.
The second was lower, set about three inches
off the floor, and slightly in front of the first.
The girls were to belly up to the first bar,
draping themselves over it, and stretching
down to grasp the lower bar, hold on tightly.

To reach the bar on the far side they were
forced up on their toes. The maneuver caused
their short blouses to ride up behind, fully
displaying the three pantied rear-ends, tight
muscular young thighs, and calve muscles
stretched taut by the strain of the demanding
pose.

The rules of the contest were simple. A
mild irritant was to be applied to stimulate
each little behind. The first girl to remove
her hands from the lower bar would lose.
Her punishment would be ten smacks on the
behind. The second to lose control would be
given five smacks. The winner would be spared
the punishment.

While she was explaining the rules, Monique
had been busy making other preparations.
She now approached the first of the three

cute rounded bottoms. In her hands she held a paint brush, a small can of some kind of liquid, and a packet of itching powder. I watched with considerable interest as she plucked the top elastic of the white nylon panties between her thumb and forefinger and carefully lowered it over the two rounded swells of a shiny adolescent butt.

Dipping the brush into the little can, she began to brush a thick syrupy liquid onto the first girl's ass, swabbing it with broad strokes up and down the jutting mounds. The tickling brush caused her to squirm a bit, but she maintained her hold. As a final touch, she ran the wet thick brush directly up the center-crease causing the girl to clench her buttocks as the bristles tickled her little asshole. The girl gave a yelp of surprise, bounding up on her straining toes, but she held on. When Monique was satisfied that she had coated the little behind thoroughly, she walked to the next victim, leaving the twisted nylon around her thighs.

Once more she repeated the process, covering the little rounded hills with gleaming syrup, tickling it deep in the dark valley between them. Then it was on to attend to the last girl, who was even now squirming a little and clenching her cheeks in anticipation. She too got the same careful, generous treatment.

Now Monique was ready for phase two. This involved spicing up the little behinds with the devilish itching powder. I later learned that the syrupy liquid was designed to hold the powder in place. Mixed with the itching powder it imparted a most virulent burning sting to the victim's behind.

Monique now went back to the first girl. Pulling on the elastic waistband, gained access to the inside of the seat of the panties, which she liberally dusted with the snowy powder. Then she hauled them up snugly into place over the sticky coated ass. With an extra tug on the elastic she made sure the nylon was embedded tightly in the girl's crotch. Next she slowly, lovingly massaged the little mounds through the thin nylon, plastering the panties firmly against the shiny rearcheeks. Once more she repeated the procedure, deliberately and thoroughly, on the other two waiting behinds.

At first I was disappointed in the results. The three stood stock still, waiting patiently. There was no sign of their being affected by the hot mixture plastered on their cute little bottoms. Then I heard a "yelp," and an "ouch," and more, as the air became filled with their howls of pain and they begged and pleaded for relief. The little asses were alive now, dancing delightfully, squirming and rolling, shaking and wildly gyrating, as the girls hopped from foot to foot, vainly seeking relief from the blazing prickly heat tormenting their soft round mounds.

It took only a few seconds for the girl on the right to jump up, her hands flying behind her to clutch her burning nylon-encased cheeks, trying desperately to rub away the terrible itch. The girl on the other end followed suit, bolting upright, her little hands rubbing furiously as the burning itch bore deeper into her soft bottom. The girl in the center lasted a second longer then she too jerked up straight to grab at her ass, joining her comrades holding their blazing little behinds, dancing and hopping about, and yelling at the top of their voices, much to the amusement of their classmates.

At last relief was forthcoming as three large, wide-mouthed pails of water were brought out. Caring not one wit about dignity, or the comic picture they presented, the girls were allowed to squat down over the buckets, sinking their firey mounds into the cool water with a collective sigh of relief.

Mademoiselle Van Daam surveyed the little scene with a contemptuous sneer. Then, with their behinds well soaked in water, she had them stand at attention before her to receive their punishment. The lucky winner was excused and allowed to take her seat, although she asked for, and was granted, permission to remain standing.

The other two girls looked a sorry sight indeed. Their hair was wild; their faces soaked in sweat. They hung their heads in humiliation, water trickling from their sopping wet panties, soaked their socks and formed two little puddles on the floor.

In order to spare herself the rigors of personally administering the punishment, Monique decided that the two would do the honors each for the other. Sobbing and sniffling, the two bedraggled females slowly walked back to the double bars to meet their fates.

The first to be on the receiving end was a skinny little brunette with long narrow legs. Her slight figure, small features, and short black hair gave her a boyish look. I studied her neat trim hips and high-set buttocks as she stepped up to the bar. Once again she assumed the position, her pink buttocks, and the dark valley separating the cheeks, was clearly visible through the wet translucent nylon.

Monique approached the other girl, a short sturdy adolescent with auburn hair cut in childish bangs, and handed her the spanking paddle. This resembled the sort of paddle used in table tennis, the flat blade covered with ribbed rubber to assure a sharper bite. She was to paddle the proffered ass with vigor, and if she wasn't sufficiently enthusiastic, the punishment would be doubled for both.

With that Monique peeled the damp clinging panties down, baring two darling little hillocks. Working the wet nylon scrap down to the thighs, she left the panties in place suspended just above the knees. Meanwhile, the girl with the auburn hair was unbuttoning her blouse and slipping it off her shoulders, so that she would have greater freedom of movement. A lacy white brassiere encasing her small firm knobs, contrasted strikingly with her deeply tanned body.

Now she stepped up to her target, reached back and delivered a stinging blow. The crisp smack echoing in the silent room. Then before the girl could recover, the paddle struck the quivering, cringing flesh again, and again, the smacking sounds mingling with her pitieous cries. Now she clenched her cheeks tightly in fearful anticipation, but the next two blows fell without mercy.

The girl was allowed a few minutes to recover, which she spent in rubbing her aching behind. Then, with Monique's permission, she pulled up her pants, took off her blouse, and took her place a little behind and to the side of the punishment bar.

Their roles reversed, the first girl surrendered the paddle and stretched her tanned compact body over the padded board, straining to reach the bar on the far side. Monique once again lowered the panties, removing the thin nylon barrier, the last protection for the vulnerable asscheeks.

Now it was the wiry little brunette who wound up and delivered a glancing blow, flattening the rounded mounds of the proffered behind, sending them wobbling and eliciting a hurt "ouch" from her sister. I watched the trembling globes reverberate, their quivering movements just beginning to subside, as they were sent shaking once again by the smack of a second blow. Three more shots followed in rapid succession. The girl screamed, hollared, and cursed, but her punishment was far from over. Having lost the little game, she was due an extra five, and these would be administered by her mistress personally.

Monique disdained the paddle, preferring the stinging cut of the riding crop. She approached the squirming rear end, now a mass of red flesh, throbbing painfully, and she caressed the smarting mounds with a leather-gloved hand. At the first touch the girl involuntarily clenched her cheeks, but when the soft caress followed she gradually relaxed them. That was what Monique had been waiting for, and she snapped the riding crop with a flick of the wrist. The hiss of the crop cutting the air ended in a vicious whack. An angry welt appeared across the reddened ass-cheeks. The girl shrieked, jerking bolt upright, and clutching at her blazing behind. Monique waited. The girl rubbed for a moment, then, in resignation, resumed her stretched position of offering. The solid thwack of the riding crop across hips and buttocks, was heard four more times. The girl was broken now, sobbing and moaning in pain, she gingerly held her punished behind until Monique released her, allowing her to rejoin the class.

* * *

Now the class was given a short break as preparations were made for the next demonstration. This involved placing a round glass table and two metal lawn chairs at the front of the room. The table was set with silverware and a tea service for two was laid on. Two of the older girls had been selected to act the parts of refined ladies taking their afternoon tea in a garden. For this skit it was necessary that they remove their skirts and panties.

This they did with practiced efficiency, dropping their skirts, skimming down their panties, and standing for inspection before their stern instructor. Their blue blazers hanging down to their hips, allowed their fuzzy netherbeards to peek out below, tucked between their slim adolescent thighs. They retained their kneesocks and shoes, in effect framing the pale naked thighs between the dark jacket and the white stockings. When they turned around one could see that the hem of their jackets covered only the top halves of their jutting behinds.

At a word from their instructor they took their seats at the table, carefully keeping their knees apart as they were told, their bare asses sitting directly on the metal chairs. The other actresses selected for this little drama were two of the youngest girls, a couple of pubescent blonds who, with eager girlish charm, scrambled to their assigned places, crouching under the table. Each was armed with a feather, and a small vial of body lotion. Their task was to provide the erotic stimulation; the two tea drinkers were to demonstrate how a lady could maintain her self-control under trying circumstances.

My eyes went to study the faces of these "ladies." One was particularly striking with her dark eyes and long black lashes, short hair, a fine aristocratic nose, high cheek bones, and a wide sensuous mouth. She had a sophisticated air about her, yet she maintained a ready smile and easy charm, at once approachable and slightly distant. The other, with blue grey eyes seemed the more serious. She also had dark hair, falling in shoulder length tresses. In her crisp blouse and dark blue blazer, she looked cool, efficient, and business-like.

As to the giggling minx under the table, they barely seemed fourteen, yet they had learned a lot about playing love games. From my vantage point I could easily see the blond on the right begin with her feather, applying it to the inner thighs of the cool, business-type with the grey eyes. The wicked tip of the feather lightly teased the sensitive inner flesh, while the young lady blithely chatted about the weather.

The grinning urchin, crouched between her thighs, now went about her work with a determined air. She began by tracing the line of the pink slit nestled between the outstretched bulge of the dark hairy pussy. Then she must have found the sensitive clitoris, for its owner suddenly squirmed in a lively wiggle. Under the table her thighs and legs were shifting uneasily, while above the table she kept up her idle chatter, although I noticed that she had gripped the arms of the chair, her knuckles whitening, as she held on tightly.

Now her little tormentor placed her other hand between the thighs to open her further up. With busy fingers she spread the cunt open and held back the pussylips while she carefully inserted the tip of the feather into the gaping cavern. I glanced up at her curious to see her expression. She was blushing prettily and a fine sheen of sweat had broken out on her forehead, as she struggled to keep her composure. I saw her mouth open in sudden surprise, and her tongue emerged to rim her lips several times as she heaved a deep passionate sigh.

Meanwhile she was becoming more flustered as, below the table, eager hands worked over her twat. The little gremlin assigned to that task had poured the silky lotion over her hands and she was giving the cunt before her a sensuous massage. She was slowly rubbing the oil into the pubic hair, along the soft inner folds, and around the clitoris, causing its owner to gasp in shocked surprise as one oily finger, then another was inserted into her hole. This chic sophisticate's face was flushed, her breasts heaving. Her hand shook as she raised her teacup, struggling with all her resources to ignore the tormenting fingers in her twat.

By now the sweet torture had made a shambles out of the tea ceremony. Both girls were caught up in the grip of passion, slumped back in their chairs, thrusting their hips foreward to meet the probing fingers wickedly manipulating their wet, silky lovenests. Their eyes were closed, their hair thrashed about as they tossed their heads from side to side, moaning in uncontrollable delight. Two naked bottoms were bouncing on the iron chairs as they humped in rhythm to the thrusting fingers driving them to an erotic frenzy.

The grey-eyed beauty, her eyes half-lidded, moaned and quivered as she raised her ass high off the chair. The little sophisticate held her body rigid, arms stiff, legs open and angled downward as a sudden violent tremor racked her frame, and she fell back into the chair joining her compatriot in the aftermath of a thundering climax.

This little scene, like the one before, had convinced me that at least one of Ironwood's ideals, that having to do with perfect self control, was an illusion. Like beauty or truth, it was something to strive for, but ultimately an elusive goal, one impossible to attain.

*   *   *

While the furniture was being removed I mentioned my opinion to Monique, who strongly disagreed. I argued that the degree of control at Ironwood could never really be attained by any human being. Monique challenged me, offering to introduce me to her star pupil, a girl named Jillian, who she maintained could control her reactions under the most trying circumstances.

Jillian was a tall willowy girl with a slender figure of gentle feminine proportions. Her long auburn hair, parted in the middle fell in straight twin folds draping the side of her pale face. She bowed her head in greeting me, her eyes dropping to my crotch as she had been taught. She waited to be commanded, quietly passive, totally submissive, and strangely detached. I had known many attractive women like her, their prettiness a little brittle, always a bit cold.

As I looked at the bent head and waiting form, Monique stepped up close behind her and, in a low murmuring voice, whispered something in her ear, peeling the blazer jacket back.

The languid woman let the jacket slip from her shoulders. Then, dream-like, her hands slowly undid the buttons down the front of her white blouse. All the while she stood staring vacantly over the heads of the silent pupils gathered on the floor in front of her. One by one the buttons came undone, the white silk parted and she slipped it down her shoulders and off her arms, to reveal a white lacy demi-bra snugly cupping a pair of firm apple-shaped breasts.

The languid hands glided next to the clasp at the side of her hip. Slowly she unzipped the skirt and bending forward, she slid it down to her ankles, stepping out of the little pile at her feet. Next she slipped off her shoes and began rolling a kneesock down her calve, balancing on one foot to pull it off. She repeated the procedure with the other stocking and they joined the little pile growing at her feet.

Stripped to bra and panties, she straightened up and paused a few seconds before reaching behind her to undo the clasp on her bra. With a shrug of her shoulders the loose flimsy straps tumbled down her arms, and her breasts were free. Her firm globes were perfectly round, like two hard little apples set high on her chest. I was surprised to see that their dark tips were fat and prominent. Centered and pointing slightly upward, on the milky mounds, the nipples seemed a little swollen.

Hypnotically, I watched her hands descend to the elastic of her plain white panties. Then, placing both thumbs in the waistband she ran a hand to either hip and skimmed the scrap of nylon down her legs in one girlish motion, revealing the thick dark thatch of a narrow triangle. Now totally naked, she stood before us, shoulders back, hands at her side, palms outward and open, waiting for further instructions.

Monique was giving the orders. "On your knees," she snapped. "Assume the basic position."

Slowly she sank to her knees, spreading her thighs, and sitting back on her heels. Her head hung submissively, the thick brown mantle hiding her features as we stood over her. It was the position the women of Ironwood had been taught to assume before a male. I had seen it my first day at Ironwood, when another passive beauty had knelt before me in this same position. It was a pose of total submission, the woman openly displaying herself to her master.

Monique looked at me inquiringly.

"Suppose we have her play with herself?" I suggested.

My whim brought instant obedience, as the

girl ran her hands from her hips on up to caress her boobs, rubbing and squeezing the firm round shapes.

"Look at me," I commanded. I wanted to watch her face, alert for the first signs of arousal. But when she looked up her expressionless eyes stared straight through me. There was no hint of passion on her calm features. Her hands seemed detached as they moulded the soft masses with a circular motion.

"Put your hands on your cunt, rub yourself off." I was growing impatient, and thought to escalate the action.

Her hands slipped between her thighs in response.

"Wait. Show us your hole first. Spread your lips and show it to us." I knew that some women found such an exhibition to be extremely erotic.

Her long fingers crept over her hips and pointed down to her pussy. With just her fingertips she stretched the slit open, revealing the glistening inner pinkness tucked in her hairy crotch. I had her lean back on her shoulders to give us a better view, holding that demanding pose, the sinews of her thighs quivering in protest until I released her. Then I had her masturbate, which she did by massaging the sensitive area around her pussylips and the tiny clitoris. After a few minutes of that, we forced her to stick a couple of fingers up her snatch, and provide a little wrist action.

During this whole performance it was perfectly quiet in the room, and we could hear a slight squishing sound as the hand pistoned up and down in her twat, but her gaze remained detached, her passive body displaying no hint of reaction to what the hand was doing to her cunt.

"That's enough." Monique intervened now. The hand stopped and the girl resumed her previous pose.

Monique suggested that we increase the stimulation using what she called "mechanical means." By this she meant a plastic, battery-powered vibrator, about eight inches long, which she pulled from a convenient cupboard in the classroom. We had the girl sit in a small chair facing us, and arrange herself draping a leg over each arm, completly exposing herself, opening her pussy to our gaze.

Then Monique approached her, the buzzing vibrator in hand, and without ceremony, inserted the plastic shaft into the waiting hole. Except for a slight wince when the dildo was shoved home, her face showed no response. Monique worked the shaft in, up and down a few times. Then she stepped back to let me have an unobstructed view, leaving the shaft buried deeply in the girl's twat, the white plastic base sticking out between the folds of her hairy pouch. The muffled buzzing coming from deep in her body was the only sound heard in the room. I noticed that the girl's hands had tightened on the arms of the chair, but except for this small sign, she seemed impervious to the tiny vibrations in her cunt.

She sat rigidly still as the droning buzzed on, her eyes remote, locked in a hypnotic gaze. I marveled at the way her mind was able to deny what her body obviously felt, but I wasn't ready to admit defeat.

I motioned to Monique to turn off the vibrator. We had her sit there, legs spread, with the plastic device nestled in her twat, while I made some arrangements with her mistress for one final test.

Then I excused myself for a quick trip back to my room. Rummaging through my suitcase, I found the little package I was looking for, a souvenir from my last trip to the orient. Slipping it into my pocket I strolled back to the classroom.

First I had the girl remove the vibrator, and stand up. I surveyed her cold hard body, tracing the lithe, gently curving lines from the soft brown hair at the crown of her head to her slender, perfectly-formed feet. Then I walked up to within a few inches of her and, placing a hand under her chin, raised her head till I could look straight into those cold expressionless eyes.

I told her that there was one final test for her to endure. That I would expect total obedience, and that she was to follow my instructions no matter what distractions might be introduced. Self-assured, almost insolent, the sober brunette stared back at me.

Then I held my hand up in front of her face, opening it to show her a small cone-shaped pellet about two inches long and an inch in diameter. It was wrapped in cellophane, which I slowly peeled away before telling her to hold out her hand. I deposited the pellet in her outstretched palm.

"This little present is just for you," I explained. "You are to shove it up your ass. Then you will stand at attention, and I don't want to see a single muscle move. Do you understand?"

"Yes, Master," the girl said in a neutral, mechanical tone.

With that she took the little cone, examining it with mild curiosity for a second, before her hands went to her behind. She shifted a little, opening her legs slightly, and bending forward just a bit as she inserted the pellet in place. I had her turn around so that I could inspect her for myself. Prying open the rubbery cheeks, I saw the base of the cone lodged firmly up her rear portal.

Then I pulled over the chair and sat down facing her. As ordered she stood at attention, her shoulders thrown back, breasts high and proud, and face set, eyes staring off into the distance.

Time passed slowly. I watched the clock on the wall as the sweep second hand made its inexorable circuit. I knew it would take a few minutes for the odd little suppository to do its devilish work.

The first sign that it was having an effect became evident when she broke out in a sweat, beads of perspiration forming on her forehead. She opened her mouth just slightly to gasp once, a sudden intake of breath.

"Not a muscle," I warned threateningly.

Her tongue passed over her lips, one, twice. I saw her bite her lower lip, two little white teeth indenting the soft pink flesh, as the burning fire in her asshole grew hotter.

I knew the effort was proving to be too much for her. A strange look crept over her face, her eyes widened, and she clenched her fists rhythmically as odd sensations began to spasm through her body. Now her mouth was opened wide, gulping air in great heaves as she struggled against the burning intensity. Her face flushed darkly; sweat running down in rivelets. The tormented woman clamped her eyes shut, clenched her jaw, and screwed up her face against the growing pain.

Then I saw the first tell-tale twitch in her hips, a tiny jerking movement, barely visible. I smiled to myself. For her, this was the beginning of the end. Now her hips were jerking violently. Then she let out a long agonized scream, and dropped to her knees, her resistance broken. Her hands flew to her burning ass as she shrieked in pain. Unable to control herself, she collapsed to the floor squirming and thrashing about, her fingers clawing between her rubbery mounds in a desperate attempt to extract the blazing point of fire. I watched dispassionately, knowing that the effects would soon be wearing off as the pellet melted. Her thrashing gradually subsided, her moans turning to deep sobs shaking her body as she broke down and cried.

Later, when the class had been dismissed, Monique asked me about the suppository I had given to Jillian. I told her of the glycerin suppositories sold in specialty shops in Hong Kong, and sometimes used to punish errant females. She asked if, on my next travels to the orient, I might pick up a package for her, as she could think of several good uses to which they might be put.

CHAPTER THREE

Good Sports

The Ironwood Sporting Society was formed several years ago as a highly-select group of sexual enthusiasts. Now numbering twelve discreet gentlemen, the society's roster was strictly limited. Membership was by invitation only, and no invitations had been extended for some time. As one of the privileges of membership, weekends could be spent at Ironwood, and three or four members were likely to be found on the grounds on any given weekend.

During the course of a Friday afternoon, various members drifted into the manor house. A few of us had agreed to meet for drinks on the veranda, overlooking the lawn at the back of the house. Alex, an old school chum from my college days, and Victor, a suave sophisticate with expensive tastes in clothes, cars, and women, were waiting for me when I arrived. I had made arrangements for two of the girls,

Lindsey and Marilee, to serve us and see to our wants as we spent an hour or two in idle conversation, sipping our martinis, and watching the sun go down over the sweeping expanse of green.

Now, as we sat on the terrace drinks in hand, the two serving girls arrived. As I had specified they had donned special costumes for the occasion. Each was sheathed in a single beige body stocking. Sheer and translucent these clinging garments shaped curves and crevices, tightly moulding feminine contours from shoulders to the snug elastic banding wrists and ankles. These outfits were designed to display the wearer's charms: the thin fabric pressing against the rounded swells of a maidenly breast, nipples clearly delineated, poking back against the straining membrane, while below, pulled into a tight crease up between the wearer's legs, the nylon tightly encased the mons veneris. Soft curlings of spingy pussyhair were clearly visible, crushed by the press of the slick fabric. The costume's scoop-neck left bare the neck and shoulders as well as the upper half of the breasts. Barefoot, our erotically-clad waitresses presented themselves for our approval.

Lindsey was the taller of the two girls. She had the body of a well-developed adolescent, healthy and tanned with sandy-colored hair pulled back in a neat pony-tail. Her softly rounded tits, with their precise pink auereoles, were plainly visible through the fine mesh. She sported a light trace of down on her plump pubes.

Marilee, a lively girl with short brown curly hair, was the younger of the two. She had a small, compact body which, like her friend's was deeply tanned all over. Little budding adolescent breasts with small brown nubs strained against the nylon mesh pulled tightly over her chest. Trim hips and slender thighs enclosed her peeping vulva with its fleece of tiny brown curls.

The men were eager by the time the girls came on the scene, and the proceedings began by having the girls display their charms for us by striking a series of erotic poses.

First, we ordered them to stand at attention, side by side, so that we could conduct a detailed inspection of their young tanned bodies. They were made to turn around and touch their toes, presenting us with two charming little asses encased in gauzy nylon and straining against the silken film. Lindsey's was heart-shaped, two gentle swells bisected by a dark shadow line. Marilee's small taut butt was more rounded in shape; a narrow deep crease nicely separating her tight little hemispheres. We had them hold that pose, all the while making lewd remarks about their obvious charms.

Next, they were obliged to turn back to back, or rather ass to ass, and then ordered to bend over from the waist with hands on their thighs. We watched as they stuck back their little bottoms to kiss one another's. The smooth flow of their supple bodies from ankles to calves to thighs to the full roundness of their jutting behinds, and on up to their hanging tits, was much admired and commented on in some detail.

Then we had them kneel down and lean over backwards with their cunts facing us, heels under their asses. Raising their hips while keeping their shoulders on the flagstone porch, their thigh and calve muscles taut, they presented their pussies for our approval. Lindsey's pouting cunt lips were prominently displayed with just the hint of pussy hair surrounding her love pouch. They seemed swollen. Marilee possessed a thin pale pink slit separating the little bulge with a hazy trace of tiny chestnut curls. We kept them like that until their legs began to tremble under the strain. Still lying on their backs, hands supporting hips, we had them extend their legs upward, waving them in the air, spreading them and scissoring them in a lewd parody of calisthenics.

Next, they were made to perform a parody of a cheerleading routine for us: a series of splits, somersaults, and cartwheels. Victor had the inspired idea of having them stand on their heads. For this trick they needed some assistance, and Alex and I offered to hold their slim ankles as they balanced, upside down, against the wall. In their pose their trim adolescent figures were well displayed, the clean lines sweeping from toes to shoulders. Their flopping little boobs stood out most prominently in the upside-down position.

Upon completing their impromptu show, we decided to separate the two, assigning each a task for which she seemed well-suited. Lindsey would provide us with a view to enhance the scenery, while Marilee would provide a little action to relieve our, now straining, hardons.

Accordingly, we sent Lindsey off to fetch the bondage paraphernalia; anklets, wrist bands, collar, and leather binding straps, that she would need. Marilee was dispatched for fresh drinks, and we made our plans.

When Lindsey returned we tied her up. With her arms at her side we encircled her nylon-clad body with thin leather straps. One was placed around her slender shoulders slightly indenting the tops of her milky globes, as Victor cinched it behind. The second strap passed just below the breasts, binding her arms tightly against her sides. The third strap, wider than the other two, was placed directly over the center of her soft shapely masses, imprisoning the nipples. This strap was cinched tightly distending her rounded shapes and squeezing her tits together as it cut into the pliant flesh. Victor had our helpless captive inhale and hold her breath as he gave a final tug on the strap.

Next, a short strap about four inches wide was snapped around her neck forming a high leather collar. From this we ran a length of rope up to a vine trellis which extended over part of the porch. The bars, framing the trellis, made an excellent anchor for the other end. Tied to one of these rafters the trussed-up female had some freedom of movement, since we had left some slack in her tether, but she

would not go very far. To restrict her further
we used an ankle spreader. This was a bar
about three feet long, which had rings on
either end to be attached via spring clips, to
the leather cuffs which fitted tightly around
each ankle. This device forced the bound figure to maintain an open-legged posture, allowing maximum exposure of her pussy. As a
final touch we blindfolded the tethered female.

Then we pushed back our chairs and sat
down to admire our handiwork, as Marliee
served the drinks. Next it was her turn to
provide the entertainment. We made her crawl
under the table. Since there were three of us
and only one of her, we decided that she
should be kept busy with both hands and her
mouth. We flipped coins, odd man out, to see
who would get her mouth. Victor won, and
Alex and I pulled our chairs around the circular table on either side of his.

Crouching down in front of Victor, little
Marilee extended a hand to either side, resting her palms on our crotches. Then she was
busy unzipping each of us, reaching in to free
our throbbing cocks. Now she was totally involved with three tumescent pricks, one in
each small hand, and one captured entirely in
her hot sucking mouth.

I felt her soft cool fingers encircle my hard
shaft, sending a thrill through my body. Grasping me tightly, she slowly moved her little fist
up and down. I sprawled back on the chair.
My eyes, half-closed, rested on the tethered
female swaying slightly in her bonds, as I

took a sip from my glass. Alex was slumped back his eyes closed in dreamy revery.

Victor ran his hands under the table to grasp the little adolescent, holding her by the face as he plunged in and out of her hot little mouth. Then she was speeding up her hand action, matching it to the rhythm of Victor's plunging hips. I closed my eyes and grunted as waves of pleasure cascaded through me. Then I was spurting my cum onto her yanking hand. Both Alex and Victor came about the same time. The three of us grunting and groaning, must have caused the blindfolded girl to wonder. Alex spilled his passion seed onto her other hand, while Victor jerked explosively and pulled his tool from her clenching lips at the last moment to send his creamy semen spurting onto her face as she tried to capture it with tongue and mouth.

She scrambled out from under the table, to stand before us. She had two sticky hands, and a sexy grin of satisfaction on her cute face which glistened with gobs of hardening cum. We also noticed a dark moist stain had appeared just at the crotch of her pantyhose. The stimulation had been getting to her, too.

It was Victor's opinion that since Marilee was such an accomplished masturbatrix, she might be made to manualize her hanging compatriot. He whispered some instruction to her now. Silently she took her place, crouching down before the blindfolded female. Then she swiftly slid a hand up a straining thigh to cup the soft folds of her friend's vulnerable sex. The girl jerked in surprise at the sudden intimate caress. We watched her twitch and squirm as Marilee palmed the opened slit. Lindsey was making soft whimpering sounds in a pleading tone as Marilee kept up the slow deep rub, massaging her stretched cunt through the nylon.

Now the hanging girl's hips began to answer the delicate teasing. She hunched forward, seeking to capture the pleasuring hand between her hungry thighs. She was rhythmically bucking her hips and straining forward as her cries rose in pitch, while the slow steady feminine hand manipulated her furry pussy.

In a moment it was over. The tormented adolescent let out a tiny whimper, and hung her head forward. The wet clinging nylon at her crotch told the story of her spent passion.

The final chapter in this little episode was suggested by the always-inventive Alex. His idea was to tie the two playmates together. For this arrangement we decided that we would bind them to one another in such a way that their supple, nylon-encased bodies would be matched; tits to tits, thighs to thighs, and pussy to pussy. We set about arranging them. First, we removed the tethering rope from the trellis overhead. Then we made Marilee step up close to Lindsey, placing her head against the older girl's shoulder.

For this Lindsey's ankle spreader was detached, and her ankles were bound together. One by one the straps were untied, only to be reattached, binding the two girlfriends together in an intimate embrace, front to front. Marilee's girlish bumps nestled against Lindsey's small round knobs. In the interest of fairness, Marilee was also blindfolded.

Satisfied with the tableau, Alex ran a hand down each girl's back. Then he stepped behind Marilee to caress her flanks. Gliding his hand across the nylon, he cupped an asscheek, squeezing, tasting its resiliency. He gave her a couple of glancing slaps on the behind, causing her to jerk forward, almost toppling the little duo, whose ankles had been tied snugly together.

He continued to play with her behind, poking a finger at the nylon stretched over her dark center crease. Marilee let out a "whoops," at the sudden intrusion in that secret place, and jerked forward sending the two of them wobbling. Alex steadied them with a hand on each ass until they regained their balance.

"Let's have them rub their titties together," Victor suggested.

Once again some adjustments in the straps were necessary, those around their upper bodies being loosened so they could comply. The randy pair shook their shoulders and pushed out their chests, forcing their little tits together in an obscene dance. We stepped closer to watch the action as Lindsey's small pink circles stirred and stiffened against the nylon barrier, and Marilee's perfectly-formed tiny dark nubs swelled and hardened in excitement.

Testing them between their legs, Victor pro-

nounced that the little darlings were both hot
and moist. They certainly were flushed with
the heat generated by their vigorous squirming. Victor whispered that the bitches needed
to be cooled off. I saw him head for the
garden hose lying against the side of the porch.

He aimed the nozzle at the blindfolded pair
and turned the tap on full. A powerful blast
of cold water suddenly struck the squirming
duo, toppling them against Alex, who lowered the howling, gasping bundle to the
ground.

Then Victor advanced on them keeping
the hose trained on whatever little behind
presented itself to him as the captives rolled
over, squirming and flopping around on the
wet flagstones. His advance was relentless and
the girls had no chance to recover from the
sudden shock, when they found themselves
being drenched by the cold stinging jet pounding against their soft young bodies.

Satisfied that the pair had been thoroughly
soaked, Victor turned off the powerful stream,
to let them recoup. The wet nylon, made
even tighter by the leather strapping, clung
to their curves like a second skin. Their hair
was plastered to their heads, and water ran
off their flushed, excited faces in rivulets. We
let them lay there in a little puddle, slowly
drying out, while we finished our drinks and
watched the sunset.

*   *   *

That evening at supper the three of us
talked about the day's events. Roger, one of

the older club members joined us, and we gave him a detailed account of our activities. We discussed how the two girls had aroused each other by mutual tit stimulation. This led the conversation to the subject of female love and lesbian activities among the residents of Ironwood.

There was no doubt that the randy, over-sexed, and constantly stimulated females of Ironwood preferred men as sexual partners, but when circumstances required it they showed no reluctance in touching, kissing, caressing, fondling and making love with their sisters. Their training had systematically rooted out and destroyed all sexual inhibitions. They had been taught to experience and appreciate human sexuality in all its varities. Thus they took the same unabashed joy in the caress of lips or hand, whether by male or female. After some discussion of this subject, we decided to have a few of the girls put on a little performance for us in the ways of Sappho later that night.

*   *   *

We sat around in the well-worn comfortable chairs of the library, which we had moved into a circular arrangement, leaving a broad expanse of deep-pile carpet free in the middle. The room had been darkened except for a pair of floor lamps set up to act as floodlights. These cast a large pool of light onto the dark burgandy carpet.

Into this light two young women silently emerged from the shadows. They were dressed in tunics and abbreviated skirts, nylons and high heels, the standard evening uniform at Ironwood. One, a tall striking blond named Jacqueline, wore a uniform of deep brown with matching tan nylons. The other was Kimberley, a cute thin girl with pretty little features and closely-cropped black hair, who was dressed in pale violet. They entered the pool of light, turned towards us, seated in the shadows, got down on their knees and bowed their heads.

Now our two lissome young performers stood up and approached each other. They embraced and they kissed, a long, lingering, slow kiss, full on the mouth. Then the blond dropped her arms to her side to stand passively as the slender brunette clasped the tab on the front of her tunic and, drawing down the zipper, revealed a long tanned body and a pair of hanging soft globes. They were the size and shape of full ripe pears. She wore no brassiere. Her breasts, unfettered, swayed slightly as she bent forward.

At Ironwood the standard uniform had several variations. For example, girls might be made to go topless, or bottomless. The options could be specified at the whim of the male, in advance of the evening's entertainment. They depended largely on personal or group preferences. Roger, who had made the arrangements for this evening, specified that the standard uniform be worn with no underwear. Thus, the braless blond.

Now Kimberley was on her knees in front

of the blond goddess. Her busy hands were at the clip on the side of the skirt, tugging the little zipper down, and working the abbreviated garment over the slim hips and down the long columnar legs. Like a statue, the blond stood rock still, allowing herself to be unveiled. When the skirt came free our eyes traveled back up the slender legs to the cloudy tuft of pale blond fuzz covering her little pubes, a soft mound tucked below the gentle curve of her belly, framed by the tan garter belt and stockings.

Next her shoes came off. Then a loving hand traveled up one of the nylon encased legs, tracing the feminine curves, until it came to the broad tight band at the top of the stocking. Garter belt clasps were methodically undone and the nylon rolled down the rigid leg. Her breasts swaying, the blond reached out to balance herself with a hand on the shoulder of the kneeling brunette, as the nylon was tugged off her toes, first one foot, then the other. The garter belt was next, falling to the floor, a tangle of lacy straps.

Jacqueline was totally naked now, standing in the halo of light. My eyes drank in her perfect body, the lithe shoulders, long flowing lines down to trim hips, and beyond down the graceful curves of her legs. Kimberley stood back to let us admire the statuesque form. Then she began her own strip-tease.

Once again she began with the tunic zipper, which this time, revealed a pair of small firm high-set breasts. They shook a little as she wiggled her shoulders, shrugging off the jacket, letting it fall to the floor. Perhaps she was eager to get started, or maybe she was simply more casual about her own undressing, but the movements over her body were quick and efficient. The skirt was undone and, with a brief tug, fell to her feet in a little heap. Her pussy was surprisingly hairy, a riot of little black curls covering the soft bulge, and spilling over onto her inner thighs. The nylons were pulled off and she was left delightfully naked.

While the brunette was almost as tall as the blond, the differences between their naked beauty was striking. The brunette's young body was firm and slender; her pale coldness seemed a little hard. By contrast the blond was deeply tanned. Her body seemed to glow with an inviting warm softness. A welcoming, come-hither feeling, radiated out from her, touching every male in the room.

Now, both totally naked, they embraced once again. As they clutched each other tightly, they sank to their knees, keeping upper body contact, maintaining a deep soul kiss, as hands roamed along backs and asses, touching, fondling the gentle curves.

Still locked in their embrace, they settled to the carpet. Laying wrapped in each others arms, they intertwined their legs, pressing pussy against thigh, tits against tits.

Then the eager brunette was on top of the languid blond. Placing a knee on either side of her hips, she straddled the supine form and, bending down, planted a kiss on her open mouth. Then, with a series of little fluttering kisses she teased her on the lips, chin, neck, and along the narrow path between her soft globes. Now she was cupping a breast, raising it reverently, to take it into her mouth. The object of all this affection seemed half-asleep, but her hips stirred, and she moaned a little as her nipple was enclosed in the hot damp cavern.

Kimberley worried that nipple, like a dog with a bone, tugging on it. Capturing the bud gently between her teeth, she moved her head from side to side. When she let it go the tip plopped free; the quivering nipple glistening in the glare of the lamps, hard and erect.

Now her black-haired lover ran her hands down the flanks and onto the hips of the stirring blond. The hands glided across to the soft vulva with its blond fleece. We saw Jackie shift her hips and open her legs to allow the probing fingers easier access.

A finger was up her cunt, then two, then three. She closed her eyes, her brows knitted in seeming concentration, as the knowing female hands caressed her, penetrating her inner recesses. Her lips parted and she breathed a long "oooh."

The moan seemed to stimulate the energetic Kimberley to even greater efforts, and she drove her hand in and out of the quivering cunt.

Tiny rhythmic squishing sounds broke the silence of the darkened room. The blond was squirming, tossing her head from side to side, flailing the carpet with her long silken strands. Moaning and sighing, she urged on her girlfriend, responding to the vigorous finger fucking with cries of "nooo," repeated again and again in a pleading voice. Then with an urgent whimper, we saw her body go rigid, as she was swept up in her orgasm. Kimberley, sensing the right moment, plunged her hand into the sopping cunt and held it there, pushing, as the straining blond came to her peak and, with a huge sigh slipped silently over the top.

Kimberley pulled her hand, wet and gleaming, from her friend's steamy twat, and examined it as if it were some strange appendage.

"Lick your fingers," Roger barked, his voice breaking the spell. "Clean them off."

She placed her hand to her mouth and ran her flickering tongue up and down the long sticky fingers. Then she sucked on two of them, cleaning her fingers thoroughly as she had been ordered to do.

With this intervention, Roger broke the charmed circle of silence enfolding the loving pair. This opened up the performance to further suggestions from the audience.

"Have them do a sixty-nine number," suggested Victor.

It was so ordered and the girls shifted to get into the mutual love position. This time slim, lithe Kimberley lay flat on the carpet, her arms at her side, while the leggy blond climbed on top, backing up to squat, her wet cunt against the pretty white face, while she strained to kiss and lick at the soft pussyfolds in front of her lips. We watched Jacqueline extend a long pink tongue and lovingly trace the vee of her friend's crotch. She bowed deeply to lick at the inner thighs, thoroughly coating the silky flesh with a sheen of her saliva. Then she placed a hand inside each thigh and pushed, opening up her lover, making her still more vulnerable to the teasing tongue.

Now she was licking up and down the pussy slit. Swollen, engorged with blood, the netherlips had blushed a dark pink. Kimberley strained her hips up in an effort to force the tantalizing tongue deeper into her hole. Then the blond was attacking with vigor. She circled the tiny clitoris, teasing it with little flicks of her tongue. Then, extending it out rigidly, she speared the open cunt, penetrating deep into the hole, running it up and down the silken walls.

The owner of the cunt responded by raising her thighs and clamping them over Jacqueline's pretty ears, as squeezing and pulling, she tried to get still more of the probing tongue into her hot quivering snatch. Both girls were making tiny sounds now, their noises muffled as their faces burrowed deeper into wet cuntmeat. We watched the muscles of Kimberley's straining thighs go taut against the blond head. Then, with hips bouncing and legs thrashing, the slim brunette came to a roaring climax.

Meanwhile, the loving Jacqueline, her work done, slowly sat up and pushed her ass further back, to let Kimberley finish her off. Now she sat upright and her hands went to her own tits, as she squashed her cunt down on the pretty struggling face beneath her crotch. We watched her face, eyes closed in ecstasy, breathing labored, as she was driven to her second shattering orgasm of the evening. Then it was over for her and she fell forward, panting mightily. The two depleted females rested there in a little heap, totally spent.

We stared, hypnotized, at the still bodies, waiting for them to stir.

"Let's punish the blond," Roger's cold voice cut like a knife, breaking our revery.

Victor and Alex went to get a low coffee table, bringing it into the circle of light. Roger ordered the girls to get up and he arranged them for a show of discipline. Jacqueline was placed on her knees, her back to us, and bent over. Her soft tits rested on the table top. We had a tantalizing view of her nicely-rounded ass as it jutted back at us, the dark amber valley neatly bisecting the twin hemispheres.

Kimberley was now handed a small whip composed of a short leather handle and ending in half a dozen thongs. She took her position behind the kneeling form and, at a nod from Roger, hauled back and struck. The air parted with a swish and the thin straps bit into the soft flesh. The shrill scream of pain surprised us. A crisscross of nasty stripes appeared on the clenching cheeks of Jackie's bottom. Again the brunette struck; again the blond cried out. Even though the blows were administered with only a light flick of the wrist, the stinging leather must have cut painfully, judging by her screams and the reddening condition of her smarting ass. After a dozen of these blows, the blond was crying and moaning piteously, begging us to have it stopped.

Roger ordered the little brunette to desist. Deep throated sobs racked her body, filling the silent room, as we stared at the well-punished ass.

"Now you must soothe her poor behind. Kiss it and tell her you're sorry," Roger ordered the brunette.

Kimberley knelt down behind the softly sobbing Jacqueline and caressed her swelling mounds. They winced at the slightest touch. Then she was licking the wounded flesh, laving the soft swells with her tongue. Slowly, lovingly, she ran her tongue up and down the warm asscheeks. Jackie let out a sigh of relief and squirmed her ass in delight.

We kept them at it for another hour, stimulating each other with games of mutual arousal, until we saw that they were hot and ready once again. Then we hurriedly stripped, clothes flying in all directions, as we joined them on the carpet. For the next few hours the two girls were kept very, very busy.

CHAPTER FOUR

City Lights

Lately I had been feeling rather harassed, totally consumed by my involvement in the world of Ironwood. I had been traveling around the globe, constantly calling on our select clientele, negotiating terms and assuring that our customers were completely satisfied with the products we delivered. On my infrequent returns, for brief stays at the manor house, I was again emersed in business matters, although I always made it a point to combine business with pleasure on those rare occasions. All in all, I felt that I needed a few days off, a little vacation completely away from it all. I decided to go to London.

I mentioned my plans to Cora who suggested that I take along one of the girls as a traveling companion. For the purpose, I selected Kimberley, the lithe brunette who had performed so admirably in the little lesbian tryst we had staged. Kimberley with her short-cropped hair, delicate features, and girlish figure, looked all of seventeen. She was a bright, lively girl with sparkling dark eyes, and the mischievous grin of a wanton street urchin. Indeed, she seemed like a little girl dressed up to play the part of a whore.

I thought about the trip with growing anticipation. I set the date and informed Cora. She would see to it that Kimberley was prepared. I left detailed instructions as to what the girl was to wear, what clothes she would be permitted to pack, and what other things I wanted included in her baggage. Then I left to pack. We were to leave at seven.

Precisely on time my little traveling companion presented herself at my door. She had been dressed in a pair of tight shorts, her slender legs bare, and her feet encased in leather sandals. The bottom of a loose-fitting white blouse had been pulled up, twisted, and tied in front to bare her satiny midriff, trim hips, and taut belly. The top three buttons of the blouse had been casually left undone, revealing the smooth skin of her neck and upper chest as well as a generous decolletage. It was obvious that she wore no bra; her dark nipples clearly visible through the thin white fabric. Pushed back on her head was a huge pair of sunglasses. Head bent, eyes lowered, she dutifully trailed after me as I went to get the car.

*   *   *

That evening we checked into our hotel

and went to our room to change for dinner. I took off my shoes and started to undress. Kimberley kicked off her sandals. Then she shimmied out of her shorts, squirming and tugging to work them over her hips. She undid the tie and the few remaining buttons of her blouse. Then, leaving the loose garment hanging on her slim frame, she reached up under it to pull her panties down and off. Now clad in nothing but the open blouse, she padded around the room, unpacking and hanging her clothes.

I was slipping off my pants while Kimberley was opening her suitcase, her back to me as she slung it onto the bed and leaned over to work the latch. As she bent over further, the bottom edge of the blouse rode up, exposing the bottoms of her pert little asscheeks.

Hurriedly, I skimmed down my briefs and, taking advantage of the opportunity, stepped up behind the bending female, placing my hard cock up along the dark shadowcrease between her rubbery cheeks. She started to straighten up, but I pushed her shoulders forward, forcing her to throw out her hands to brace herself on the bed.

Then I ran my hands around the front of her thighs, over her flat belly and on up to clasp her loosely hanging boobs. Small and round, they dangled like two little pears, ripe for the picking. I cupped my hands around those luscious fruits, and gave her a friendly squeeze, all the while grinding my hips into her ass, feeling her up while her smooth mounds pressed against my hips and her warm crack caressed my rigid prick. She clenched her cheeks, imprisoning me, and made some delightful little movements with her ass.

I left her standing there with orders not to move. Retrieving my traveling kit and I found a jar of vaseline. Slowly, I greased my throbbing shaft while admiring the rounded contours of Kimberley's tight-cheeked young bottom. Approaching the proferred behind, I pried open her rearmounds and dabbed a glob of the gel right on her dimpled asshole. At first the tiny gate resisted my poking finger, but then my finger slipped in and she sighed as I diddled her in that most intimate spot.

Now I moved to replace my finger with my straining cock, placing the head directly on the tiny roseate and pressing till the tight ring of rubbery flesh yielded and the crown of my cock was snugly inserted up her bottom. Slowly I eased into the tight-fitting channel until I was about halfway in, then, with a furious thrust I buried myself up to the hilt, getting a passionate cry from the impaled female.

I grabbed her dangling tits, holding onto them like handles as I pulled back and lunged all the way back in. She met my long deep thrusts with movements of her own, straining backwards, jutting out her ass, and pushing against my churning hips. Her tight little asshole clenched my prick, sending delicious sensations coursing through my body. I pulled on her tits, mauling them roughly as I rode her to an exploding climax, pumping my semen into her churning behind.

I pulled away and left her standing there in the bent over position, cautioning her not to move. I sat down with a cigarette, studying her still figure, the lovely swells of her upturned ass, the thin girlish legs, the wet sheen on the inside of her thighs telling of her spent passion. When I finished my cigarette, I smacked her on the haunch, and told her to get dressed. I was getting hungry.

*   *   *

For dinner that evening, Kimberley had donned a black sheath dress with matching black opaque nylons. Her dress left bare a generous expanse of neck and soft shoulders, the low cut front revealed the top contours of her breasts. In order to constantly remind her of her bondage to Ironwood, I had her wear a wristband. This was not the thick, serviceable type of strap used in the punishment cell, but rather the thinner decorative type used on special occasions. It was made of shiny patent leather with tiny silver studs set along each edge. The gleaming black leather tightly encircled her pale white wrist.

We sat in a deeply curved booth in the elegant dining room of the hotel. Kimberley looked lovely in the soft light, her dark eyes deep and sensuous. As we sipped our drinks I let my hand rest on her leg, rucking up her dress so I could freely run my hand up and down the smooth column of her nylon-encased thigh. Her flesh felt warm and moist through the gauzy sheath. I had an idea.

"Kimberley, I want you to take off your panties," I said directly.

She smiled at me and without hesitation, as though it was the sort of request she got often, she raised her hips and reached under her dress to pull her panties down to her knees. She looked around now, concerned at what the other diners might have seen. But they were ignoring us.

"Go on take them off . . . all the way. I want them."

She bent a little to one side and bringing her leg up, tugged the twisted nylon down and off her foot. Then she raised the other knee and reaching down retrieved the little garment which was hung up for a moment on her high-heeled shoe. She handed the crumpled nylon over to me without a word. It was still warm from her body. Through all of this her eyes had never left mine. I looked deep into her eyes and held the panties to my nose, inhaling deeply, then I crumpled them and stuffed them in my jacket pocket.

Next I had her pull up the tight dress. She worked the material up several inches exposing the tight wide bands at the top of her stockings.

"All the way," I insisted.

I wanted her to sit there with her bare ass directly on the leather seat of the booth. Towards that end she had to work the slinky material all the way to her waist. In the shadows under the table, I could see her bare thighs and the hint of the darker shadow between them. I looked over at our fellow diners, wondering how much they could see under our table. Now she had the material out from under her and she was squirming on the leather.

"Now you are to go to the ladies room and remove your brassiere. Bring it back to me."

She did as I had ordered. When she returned she slid back into the booth, passing a little tangle of lacy straps under the table, her freed breasts swaying as she bent towards me. I laid a hand firmly on her naked pussy, not moving, but only resting it there, her heat against my palm.

"Now listen to me, Kimberley. This is how I want you. For the rest of this trip you're not to wear panties or bra without my permission. Moreover, just as tonight you wear the band of Ironwood on your wrist, so you will always have some symbol of your bondage, your subjugation, on your body. You may be away from Ironwood, but you'll never escape Ironwood. You have been selected as one of the chosen few to be granted the privilege of receiving training in the Ironwood tradition. You must be proud, and you must never forget. Do you understand?"

She looked deep into my eyes, a look of subjugation and sexual desire. Her long lashes fluttered down and she nodded her head in docile submission.

"Now I have something for you." I reached into my pocket and pulled out a small dildo of soft rubber.

This novel love toy was banana-shaped and filled with mercury. The surface was covered with small ridges which could be expanded by the shifting liquid. Whenever the wearer moved, it shifted within her, creating the most delightful sensations, or so I had been told.

"You're going to stick this up your twat," I explained. "Then, we're going to relax, and have a nice, slow leisurely meal. And you will sit there with your bare ass on the leather, wearing this little toy up your cunt as a constant reminder of who you are. More wine, my dear?"

I watched her delicate fingers close on the rubber shaft, squeezing and testing it with curiosity. She slid back on the seat, spreading her thighs. Then with her left hand she reached down to open herself, and holding her cunt lips apart, gently inserted the dildo. I watched it slide up into her, and her thighs close around it. She shifted a little to accommodate the bulk. She was still squirming uncomfortably, an expression of concern on her features, when the waiter arrived to take our order.

She sat there for the entire meal with the little plug constantly stimulating her, filling her sex, keeping her simmering at a low level of arousal, reminding her. She did her best to ignore the little probe, but the slightest movement, the least shifting of her weight, would cause her to bolt upright, her eyes widening in startled surprise at some unexpected thrill deep in her core.

When we got back to our room I yanked

off her dress, pulled out the dildo, and fucked her right there on the floor. Kimberley was consumed with animal lust. Her nyloned legs clenched my waist, her high heels drumming on my ass, as she wildly urged me on, in a long hard pounding fuck.

* * *

I awoke early the next morning and decided to go for a morning stroll before breakfast. Kimberley was still asleep when I crept out of the room closing the door softly behind me.

The air was crisp and light. It had rained the night before, and the city seemed cleansed. I stopped at a local cafe for a cup of coffee and lingered over the morning newspaper. Then I sauntered back to my hotel room.

When I opened the door I saw my little charge was still asleep. Once again she reminded me of a girl-child, so soft and young, and vulnerable. She lay on her side, her head cradled on one bent arm, one knee flexed, her cute rounded ass jutting towards my side of the bed. I paused to consider the invitation, but decided instead to wake her up.

I shook her shoulder gently and told my groggy playmate it was time for breakfast. She emerged from the shower, pink and freshly-scrubbed and humming a little tune, as she sat down to apply her makeup. When the bellhop knocked with our tray, I let her grab a silk robe, but it came right off again when he left the room. I wanted her to eat in the nude, sitting across from me with her firm rounded titties with their two dark centers staring at me, as I finished my eggs. As we ate I told her of my plans for the day.

* * *

Kimberley had not been to London, since she was a child and she wanted to see all the tourist spots. I had arranged for a tour of the city on one of the sightseeing buses that made the loop through central London. She dressed casually, pulling a loose, scoop-necked blouse over her naked form, and stepping into a wide billowy skirt. Since I insisted on high-heels she would have to wear nylons. Kimberley selected a beige pair with wide elastic topbands, the modern kind which would stay in place with no need for an inconvenient garterbelt. I watched as she took a seat pulling the hem of the skirt up till it crossed her thighs. Bending down she drew stockings up her shapely legs, straightening the topbands around her thighs and brushing the skirt back down into place. Then she stood up and, stepping into a pair of heels, announced that she was ready to go. She wore no panties, of course. We walked, arm in arm, down the hotel hallway.

The tourbus was waiting in the Hotel parking lot. We found seats in the rear. Kimberley promptly pulled her skirt out from under her so she sat bare-assed on the leather seat. I pretended not to notice, but I couldn't help smiling to myself.

Soon she was caught up in the excitement of the trip, chatting away, like the other eager tourists packed into the bus crawling its way through London.

It was a long day, trooping off the bus to see some castle or museum piece, and trooping back on for a hot dusty ride to some bridge or statue. We had undergone that routine several times now, and had one more stop to make before we headed back to the hotel.

On this stop I waited until all our fellow travelers had departed. When Kimberley got up to follow, I noticed there was a damp spot on the leather seat where she had been sitting. Suddenly, I had to have her. I grabbed her by the wrist as she turned to leave, pulling her back into the seat. Hungrily I shoved the skirt up and clamped a hand to her sex, my fingers in her crease, my palm against her lovemound. She was hot and moist.

Then, I whispered what I wanted her to do. Without hesitation, Kimberley squeezed back into the seat, climbing between my legs, and getting down on her knees, while I tore open my pants to release my throbbing cock.

Now she eagerly attacked the massive hardon which, suddenly freed, sprung to attention before her eyes.

She gripped me firmly, yanking her hands up and down the shaft, before licking along its length, and finally slipping my rod into her mouth. She tongued me and sucked me vigorously. Her velvety tongue whirled and stabbed and tickled, sending waves of passion rocketing through me.

We heard voices signaling that our group was about to return. I reached down and, holding her head in place, pulled out my cock just as I shot a spurt of cum into the air, and onto her pretty little face. She jerked her head back in surprise, but I held on to her by the cheeks as I hosed her face with jets of hot milky semen. She closed her eyes taking it all, gobs of cream hung on her lips, and cheeks, and eyelids.

Then the bus door was opening, and I released her. She scrambled up onto the seat, and reached for the pack of tissues in her handbag. Weakly, I tucked myself back in and zipped up my pants, while Kimberley wiped the sticky goo off her hands and face.

As the others filed onto the bus, a few seemed to glance at us suspiciously. I could only smile back contentedly. Kimberley, her hair disheveled, her makeup a mess, and a telltale smear she had missed at the corner of her lips, sat motionless her head held high, regally ignoring their stares.

The ride back had excited both of us. We rushed back to our room, tearing our clothes off. Kimberley was wet and hot, her body throbbing with excitement. She clamped herself to me, grinding her body into mine, pleading in a little girl's voice to be fucked.

I almost took her then and there, but at the last moment, I grabbed her by the hand and pulled her after me into the bathroom. We stepped into the shower together. The warm, stinging spray felt heavenly after our hot dusty afternoon. We kissed under the stinging rain, as I rubbed my cock against her belly.

Then I handed her a large cake of soap and, turning my back to her, said "Do me."

She started at my shoulders. Her soft warm hands felt lovely as she massaged little circles of suds around my shoulder blades. Her hands descended down my back. She knelt behind me to soap my butt, spending a lot of time there. I bent over, holding onto the taps, to give her better access. I was thrilled when a soapy finger ran up my crack, and she teased my asshole.

Then she had a finger in me, slipping it up my ass and screwing it around inside. I almost came, but not wanting that just then, I reached back to remove the tormenting finger. Obediently, she continued on down slowly caressing the backs of my thighs and calves.

Thoroughly soaped up in back, I turned to let her work on my front. She stood up on her toes to kiss me and, with a little grin, grabbed my cock in her hot soapy hands. Again I had to stop her. I wanted to prolong my pleasure, and she knew how to do it.

So reluctantly, she gave me up for the moment and went back to my neck and shoulders and over my chest, playing with the hair, drawing little swirls in the lather. Then she ran down my front, soaping my stomach, carefully avoiding my too-ready cock, and doing the front of my thighs and legs. Now I could hold out no longer. I placed her hot soapy hand back on my shaft, and leaned back against the wall, letting her do whatever she wanted. What she wanted to do was administer a firm, vigorous hand job. I came in huge spurts, the cream mingling with the lather on her pumping hand.

*   *   *

After dinner we spent a quiet evening in our room. Sipping drinks and toying with one another's body in a night of slow, gentle lovemaking.

The next day was the final one of our little jaunt. I had a few acquaintances to look up. Kimberley asked if she could spend some time strolling through the streets, looking at the shops. I allowed her that, specifying only that she wear wrist bands on both arms. For the rest, she was to dress comfortably, sans panties. We would meet for supper; I had a surprise planned for later that evening. And so we went our separate ways.

*   *   *

We were lingering over our coffee in the hotel dining room, when I told Kimberley of the night I had planned. I intended to take her to a very exclusive club in Soho, The Archery Club. Its members were artists, musicians, actors, and a sprinkling of professionals. Once a month they had a party to which selected outsiders were invited, provided they brought a willing female companion. Kimberley, being an Ironwood resident, was always most willing.

Back in our room I explained that for this occasion, she was to be exotically dressed in nylon and leather. First, I had her shower, brush her hair, and apply her makeup. Then I supervised her dressing.

First, panythose, shiny black, and translucent. From the waist down she would be naked except for the smoky nylon sheath and wickedly high stiletto-heeled shoes. Next, I gave her a package and let her open it. It contained a black leather jacket I had bought for her that day. She was to wear it over her naked torso. The jacket came just to her waist. The leather, lined with silk, fitted snugly, moulding her breasts. I lowered the tab of the broad silver zipper down the front, revealing the tops of her breasts and providing a generous view of the innercurves. Her nipples were already stiffening in anticipation.

Sitting on the bed, she bent over to slip her feet in the high-heeled sandals, reaching down to buckle the ankle straps. When she straightened up I was standing over her, a wide leather dog collar in my hands. Submissively, she stretched forward, offering me her neck, her eyes closed, while I buckled the collar in place.

Not wishing to be arrested on our way to the event, I wrapped her in a large loose raincoat. This would cover her from her neck to her calves. Except for the collar, she would look like any other young lady out for a walk with her date on a rainy night in London.

Outside the hotel we got a taxicab. If the driver noticed the collar, he gave no sign of it. I gave him the address and settled back, my hand resting on Kimberley's warm silken thigh, as the taxi crawled off into the night.

*   *   *

When we got there the party was in full swing. Standing in the doorway, it was hard to see clearly because of the dark shadows, colored lights, and mist of smoke that hung in the air. The air smelled sweetly, and from somewhere soft, sensuous flute music snaked through the room. Everywhere there were characters in bizarre costumes at various stages of dress and undress. I noted that many of the women were topless.

I removed Kimberley's raincoat, and clipped a light chain to her collar. Then, wrapping the other end around my wrist, I led her on this short leash, down the steps and into the crowd. As I had hoped, we made a dramatic entrance. Some of the babble of conversation stopped as guests turned towards us with appreciative stares and lewd remarks; me leading and the girl on the chain a few feet behind. As we passed among them I glanced back at Kimberley. She was maintaining her cool, ignoring the crowd, the calm poise instilled at Ironwood remained, even when furtive hands reached out to grab a feel of her silken behind.

Much of the rest of that evening remains a blur. I remember the many men who came around asking for an introduction to my little captive. I remember an older blond woman who stopped to talk to us, all the while fondling Kimberley's ass. Kimberley ignored her. There was much feeling, and touching, and caressing as clothes were gradually shed. Kimberley's jacket had been opened down the front, the leather flaps hung loosely, draping her pale body and the firm rounded tits with their pointing nipples.

At one point I let an artist-type borrow Kimberley, I being rather busy with a tall blond clad in nothing but a pair of white shorts and high heels. Sometime after that a full-scale orgy developed, and my images from that point on, are of twisting arms and twining legs, tits and asses, and bodies squirming on the floor, in every conceivable combination.

*   *   *

The ride home was quiet. It was late and Kimberley's head rested on my shoulder. We rode in silence as the taxi sped through the deserted streets. We were both exhausted, and all fucked out, as we wearily pulled off our clothes and fell into bed. That night, as I lay there savoring Kimberley's soft warmth snuggled against me, I drifted off to sleep, thinking of Ironwood.

CHAPTER FIVE

Mr. Seven Pays a Call

When we got back to Ironwood, we found that things were somewhat disrupted by the unexpected arrival of one of our best clients, a certain Mr. Seven, whose empire extended far and wide from his base in the South China Sea. When I called on him during my trips to the Orient, it was usually at one of his business offices in Singapore. Only once was I invited to his home. On that occasion he had his helicopter pick me up and deposit me on his palatial estate, situated on his own private island, far out to sea.

Mr. Seven was said to be fabulously wealthy, with diverse business dealings, some legitimate, some not. In spite of his westernized name he was of Chinese extraction, tall for an oriental, and about 60 years old, although it was difficult to judge his age. He seemed ageless.

Mr. Seven had always been a highly-valued client of Ironwood enterprises. He took a particular fancy to western women, although he sadly conceded that they lacked the essential submissive quality of oriental girls. Because of this predilection, Mr. Seven was especially pleased with our Ironwood graduates, who, in his opinion, combined the best of both worlds. Here was the blend of western glamor and eastern submissiveness, that he found so appealing.

We met in the sitting room of the manor house, where Cora and he had been discussing business when I arrived. He too, had been in London, and decided to make a detour to Ironwood on his way home.

We shook hands and exchanged pleasantries. He presented a woman he referred to as his secretary, a Miss Tai. She had a slender willowy figure, slim-hipped and small breasted, with long straight black hair, delicate features, and hands with long sensuous fingers, soft hands, one of which rested in mine for a brief moment. She bowed demurely upon being introduced, her eyes averted.

Mr. Seven was, among other things, a true sexual connoisseur. An avid devotee of Eros, he could spend hours conversing about sexual techniques, devices, and apparatus. And he had the money to indulge his passions. Knowing of my similar interests, we often shared ideas. As a matter of fact, he had with him a device he was most eager to show to me.

He snapped his fingers and Miss Tai came over holding open a fine wooden box. Inside, nestled in the silk lining, was a set of six small plastic eggs. Taking one from its cradle, Mr. Seven unscrewed the two halves to reveal the inner workings, a maze of tiny electronic parts. It contained, he explained, a tiny receiver and a vibrating mechanism.

He had been talking to Cora when I arrived about staging a little demonstration with his latest toy. It was a Saturday, and often on weekends, if the girls had no other duties to perform, they were sent out into the many flower gardens around the house, for some light yardwork.

As we drove up I noticed three of them were working out in front. They were dressed in their work clothes: denim shorts, loose blue workshirts, and sneakers. One, a young blond, had her hair tied behind in a pony-tail, as she knelt working industriously with a trowel. The other two were older and taller. Both had long tresses of soft brown hair, also tied back. They could have been sisters. They were busy pruning and shaping the shrubbery.

We stopped to look down on them from the front steps. Cora, who was also very interested in seeing the demonstration, called the girls over. Mr. Seven stood behind her. Miss Tai, holding the box, waited patiently. The girls stood below us, with their heads lowered as they were introduced.

Cora told them that the foreign gentleman had brought with him certain devices which we wished to see demonstrated. For this purpose they were to remove their shorts and panties and sit down on the steps.

Puzzled, but too familiar with the ways of Ironwood to question an order, they moved to comply. They stripped with the casual matter-of-fact manner that I had come to know so well, baring their bodies with that total lack of embarrassment outsiders found somewhat disconcerting. Without ceremony they worked on clasps and zippers, bending and wriggling to tug denim shorts down their hips. With the same easy nonchalance three pairs of panties followed to be discarded with the denim at their feet. Then they sat back on the sun-splashed steps, their bare asses on the warm concrete, arms braced behind them, awaiting further instructions.

Cora bowed to Mr. Seven, who, in turn, motioned to his assistant. She selected an egg, and approaching one of the auburn haired beauties, knelt down before her.

"Spread your knees, Miss. Open yourself up for us," Cora commanded.

The widening thighs revealed a thicket of auburn curls, the center seam a dusky pink furrow. Almost reverently the oriental girl placed a hand on the exposed slit, using her fingers to delicately pry back the lips so she could gently insert the mysterious egg. The girl watched in wide-eyed fascination as the plastic ovoid disappeared up her twat. With a final poke the egg slipped in all the way, the lips closing over it. The startled girl gasped, a

sharp intake of breath, jerking her hips reflexively at the sudden intrusion.

Meanwhile Miss Tai had gone to perform
the same bizarre ritual on the young blond,
who opened her thin girlish legs apprehensively. The oriental girl worked with well-
practiced efficiency. We watched her place a
hand on the smooth inner thigh of the blond,
easing her open just a bit more. A thin knowing hand nosed through the light sprinkle of
pale blond curlings, the blood red fingernails
strangely erotic as they dug into the soft folds
of the blond pussy. The egg was duly inserted and the fleshy lips snapped shut around
it. The surprised blond drew up her knees,
and brought a tentative hand down to lightly
touch her pussy as if to assure herself.

Now Mr. Seven's able assistant knelt before
the last girl, the bulging purse of her vulva,
like her sister's, was covered with fine dusting
of light brown curls. Once more cuntlips were
delicately parted. Once more the ovoid inserted. Once more lips clamped shut as the
egg popped up the cunt.

Now all three girls were told to put their
clothes back on and return to work. They
were to carry their little "presents" stuffed up
their cunts until they were given permission
to remove them.

The girls stood up and dressed slowly. Tentative, they moved gingerly at first, testing
their movements to see what effects the strange
eggs might have. Soon they adjusted to the
constant stimulation, merely accepting it, as

they had learned to accept so many things that were done to them at Ironwood. They stepped into their panties, pulled up their shorts, and walked back to the garden; still a bit apprehensive, although this was hardly the first time they had had to accede to some bizarre request.

We went back to the sitting room with its splendid view of the garden. Through the window we watched as our amateur gardeners took up their tools, returning to work and chatting among themselves. An occasional hand touched a crotch as if checking for something.

Mr. Seven was now busying himself with an attaché case he had placed on the table. Inside, were a set of knobs, numbered one through six. He extended an antenna out of the top of the case, flipped a switch, and watched a red light answer.

Our esteemed client invited us to observe the working girls closely, as he twisted one of the knobs. Suddenly, the little blond dropped her shovel and her head jerked back, a look of shocked surprise on her cute face. Her eyebrows shot up, eyes widening in startled response, as she let out a whoop and hollar. Mr. Seven quickly turned the knob off.

The other two had dropped their tools and excitedly rushed over to the blond. They were plying her with questions, to which she just shook her head, puzzled by the sudden flood of sensations radiating from her twat. As they clustered around her, the little blond again exploded into a flurry of movements. Caught in mid-sentence, her hands flew to her crotch as she bounced and jerked, gyrating, and hopping from one foot to another.

I glanced at Mr. Seven, who wore the intense look of a mad scientist, turning knobs and throwing switches hurriedly. At his silent command the other two girls also jerked upright as the little toys, buried deep in their twats, came to life. The garden was the scene of frenzied activity as the girls danced and jumped and hopped, their hands clutching their stimulated pussys. Now the two brunettes were kneeling, jerking their hips rhythmically, while the little blond girl lay on her back, spasms shaking her body, her legs thrashing, her hands rubbing her crotch in a bizarre parody of masturbation.

Our honorable client snapped off the power, and the frantic movement slowed and then stopped. Stunned, the three gardeners sat on the ground, legs sprawled open, still a bit dazed, and gasping for breath. Their remote tormentor let them rest a while, then he flicked his wrist again, and I saw the little blond bounce, her hips bucking forward.

She was a comical sight sitting there, her legs spread, her hips bouncing, while she tried to tug her pants down to get at the vibrating egg. But she never got the chance. Pausing to let her work her shorts down, and yank her panties to her knees, Mr. Seven let her have it again. She bounced, clutched her pussy, and rolled over on her belly, flopping around bare-assed in the dirt, her shorts at her ankles, panties twisted around her thighs.

Then the other two had joined in with wild gyrations of their own. We roared with laughter at the sight of the three girls dancing like puppets, their strings pulled by the remote puppeteer. We were still laughing at the comic sight, as the girls made desperate attempts to get at the teasing eggs vibrating deep in their cores. Then, after amusing us for several more minutes, Mr. Seven turned off the power. He calmly closed the case, and handed it to his assistant.

Through the window we saw the burst of activity subside. The three girls lay on the ground grass, panting and gasping for air. Their faces were flushed with the excitement; hair and clothes disheveled. Sitting up they looked around apprehensively, wondering what might happen next.

*   *   *

That evening an elegant meal had been laid out for our guests. Mr. Seven was in the best of spirits, as Cora and I joined him and his ever-present companion in the dining room. Miss Tai was stunning. A narrow sheath of fine white silk clung to her willowy curves moulding her slim hips and superb ass. Sleeveless, the dress had a high tunic collar and a daring slit up the side. Her only jewelry was a single gold slave bracelet fitted tightly around her slim upper arm. She smiled politely but I felt she seemed unusually tense.

Over coffee we talked about the fiendish

vibrating eggs. It turned out that one of our guest's many enterprises was a plastics factory that made vibrators. He took a keen interest in that operation, insisting on personally supervising the field testing of all the new products. Miss Tai, he told us, often participated in these tests, and she had been made to wear the egg on several occasions. In fact, he confided, she had one up her cunt at the very moment.

We turned to look at the oriental girl, but she had her head bowed, eyes averted, her pretty features masked by the black helmet of silky hair. Her master ordered her to bring his black case.

Placing a chair beside his own, he set the case on it, opened it up, and extended the aerial. Miss Tai had resumed her seat on his left, directly across the table from me. Mr. Seven dropped his hand down to the case, and we heard the snap of the powerswitch.

We waited for a reaction on the part of the submissive oriental girl, but nothing happened. Still, Mr. Seven was a very patient man. He enjoyed the slowly rising excitement growing in the room, clearly savoring the anticipation, as his beautiful assistant sat with her head down, waiting for the first vague feelings of stimulation deep in her sex.

Casually, he reached for a cigar, and took a long time lighting it. He settled back contently, resting his hand once again on the little knob, hidden from our view by the tabletop. Now he was talking about the pleasure houses of

Bangkok, and of some most unusual shows he had seen performed there.

Suddenly, the girl shot upright, a tiny "ooh" escaped from her pursed lips, and her brow knitted in surprise.

Mr. Seven grinned wickedly. He explained that while Miss Tai might seem somewhat distracted by the tiny sensations, she secretly loved the little egg tucked away in her love purse. With that the girl gave another reflexive jerk accompanied by a little squeak as if to punctuate his sentence.

Mr. Seven ignored her reaction. I refilled his cognac glass as, drawing on his cigar, he returned to his discourse on Bangkok. For the next hour we sat at the table chatting about many subjects. Our guest had a fascinating repertoire of experiences which he enjoyed relating. Throughout the conversation, at odd intervals, a spasm would shoot through the girl across the table from me, and she would squeal with a startled jump, caught by surprise.

"Miss Tai, put your hands on the table and please do not move them," he said, looking at Cora all the while.

I watched the long sinuous fingers with their gleaming red tips, curl over the edge of the table, gripping it tightly, pressing into the white tablecloth.

She sat with her eyes closed. Her long black lashes fluttered, and I saw the tension in her arms and hands as a startled response jolted her shoulders and ran through her slender frame. We watched her wriggle as tiny spasms worked their way from her shoulders to her hips. Then she started bouncing slightly in her chair, while the vibrator sent queer sensations coursing through her body. Her breath came in a series of short, quick gasps. The fingers tightened their grip on the edge of the table, whitening under the strain.

After a few seconds she was allowed a brief respite. Her shoulders slumped forward, and her head hung loosely, as she sat there, her breath coming in low gulping heaves. Her employer gazed at her and nodded approvingly, obviously impressed.

"There is one more product that Miss Tai has consented to test for us. This one she does not enjoy quite so much," he explained to us.

"Miss Tai, you will please lean over," he requested politely.

The girl leaned forward, tilted slightly towards him. The movement brought her small pointy breasts into reach. Slowly he brought a hand up to clamp it over her right breast, squeezing her, crumpling the thin silky fabric as he closed his fingers, crushing her breast in his grip.

The girl let out a shrill shriek her face contorted in agony, as tears welled up in her dark eyes. Cora and I looked at each other. The dramatic reaction took us by surprise.

"Resume your seat, Miss Tai." The oriental master was giving orders now.

The shaken girl slowly pulled herself up,

and slumped down in the chair, breathing heavily.

"Put your hand on your left breast," he ordered.

As in a dream the girl obeyed. The long fingers crept up and over the little bump in the silk.

"Now squeeze yourself," he commanded.

We watched her as the blood-red talons closed clenched on a silken mound. Her eyes were closed and her forehead creased as in intense concentration, as she punished herself. She whimpered softly, involuntarily.

"Enough." Her stern Master snapped out the word.

"These people will want to see your brassiere now. Show it to them," his voice was, once again, soft and polite.

The girl reached behind her to run the zipper of her dress down, and leaning forward, let the silk fall from her shoulders. We saw that she wore a most unusual brassiere. It was made of white latex rubber, and tightly encased her little globes, her tiny dark nipples straining against the elastic. Again her hands went behind her, and the ingenuous contraption fell forward down her slender arms landing in her lap in a tangle of elastic rubber straps and cups. Her small breasts were covered with a mass of angry red indentations.

The girl sat topless now, her dress down to her waist, her small tortured tits revealed to our eyes. Mr. Seven retrieved the bra and passed it over for my inspection.

The insides of the cups were lined with a series of hard rubber nubs. Like tiny rubber teeth, they would press, but not puncture, the soft flesh of the imprisoned breast. It would be constantly uncomfortable for the wearer under normal circumstances, but if pressure were applied, and the little nodes pressed into the vulnerable flesh, the bite could be vicious.

Cora, intrigued by the possibilities, asked Mr. Seven if she might have a few of the contraptions sent round for our experimentation. He graciously consented. We let the girl sit there with her punished little boobies hanging out, while we finished off our cognac.

* * *

From our conversation that night and subsequently I discovered that our distinguished client had a predilection for latex. I myself had never been too keen on that material preferring leather, silk, and nylon; but he was, after all, a guest, and at Ironwood, a guest's slightest wish must be gratified.

Thus it was that Cora and I decided to arrange a little entertainment for our esteemed guest, one that we hoped, he would find amusing. For this show we would need the services of three young ladies. We decided to use the girls who had entertained us earlier that afternoon with their antics in the garden.

Accordingly, the three were ordered to present themselves at the demonstration class-

room. Although it was well into the evening,
Cora specified that they wear dayclothes, the
Ironwood schoolgirl's uniform, with high heels.

I escorted our guests to the classroom where
we were met by Monique Van Daam, who
would supervise the session, Cora having excused herself to attend to other business. The
Mademoiselle was dressed, like her superior,
all in black: riding pants, boots, turtleneck
sweater, and the ever-present riding crop.

The room was dark. The only lights being
those at the front of the room directly over
the infamous double bars, scene of the chas-
tisements of hundreds of schoolgirl behinds.
This place was steeped in tradition. We took
our seats in the shadows facing the dreaded
bars.

When the hesitant trio entered the room,
Monique had them take their places under
the lights. Then she introduced them to us.
One of the brunettes' name was Dawn, the
other's Heather; the little blond was Odette.
Each went to her knees and bowed as her
name was called.

As they stood there under the lights facing
us, Monique orchestrated a little striptease.
School blazers were carefully removed, folded
and set on the floor beside them. Then they
worked on their white blouses. I was watching
the one called Dawn, as she slowly unbut-
toned the cuffs, and the front, tugged the
material free of her skirt, and pulled it off
her shoulders and down her long arms, in
one graceful motion. The white cloth flut-

tered to the floor to land on top of the jacket. This left the girls clad in very skimpy white brassieres, loose mini-skirts, kneesocks, and black high heels.

Next the skirts were ordered removed. The girls attacked the side clasps and zippers with practiced fingers and, tugging the waistbands over their hips, the three loose garments dropped simultaneously, falling down thin girlish legs to ring their ankles. They stepped out of them, and the skirts joined the growing pile of clothes at their sides.

At a word from their mistress the three reached back to the clasps of their lacy white brassieres. Soon the straps were undone, falling away, leaving us the sight of three luscious pairs of young breasts. Panties were removed next, the girls quickly slipping the white nylon down their tanned legs and stepping out of the silky pool at their feet. Shoes and socks were removed last, although Monique had them put the high heels on again almost immediately.

Now they stood before us completely naked except for the black high-heeled pumps. Monique posed them for us, hands on hips, legs spread, shoulders thrown back, head held high: totally open for our inspection.

On the left stood Dawn. Tall and well-built, her auburn hair fell in a soft mass to caress her shoulders. Her full rounded tits, with their darkened centers, hung invitingly. Her prominent vulva, covered in brown fur, stood out brazenly from her outthrust hips, as she posed proudly, legs spread, open to the world.

Next to her stood little Odette. Smaller than the other two, she had a girlish figure and the face of innocence. Her compact hips and straight thin legs were sleekly streamlined, lacking the rounder feminine curves of the other two. With her narrow blond triangle she seemed vulnerable and especially appealing. Her breasts were high and sexy, with little pink nipples peeking shyly out. Like the other two she stood with hands on hips trying to assume a brazen pose, although in her case, without much success.

Heather stood on the right. Under the lights her hair glowed with a soft brown sheen. Her body was fuller than the other two, her feminine curves more mature. Her breasts were medium sized, firm and rich, with wide dark aureoles and well-defined nipples, slightly distended. Her pussy was generously covered with a rich thatch of golden brown which darkened as it thickened between her athletic thighs. With her statuesque body and long dancers legs she was best equipped to carry off the pose of brazen femininity that Monique had tried to create.

I looked over at Mr. Seven. He had his hand in the lap of his secretary playing between her legs, as they studied the details of the naked female bodies displayed before us.

Now Monique, acting as mistress of ceremonies, brought out the special panties that we had decided would be suitable for this occasion. These were made of latex, the front and crotch composed of a translucent, milky thin membrane. But it was the seat of the panties that was of special interest. Rather than a solid piece of material these were composed of a sort of net of rubber strands. These elastic bands were cross-hatched, and would be stretched tautly against the ass once the wearer had tugged them into place.

Monique had the girls step into the rubber panties and pull them up tightly. She assured this by going to each and giving an extra tug upward on the waist band. The rubber stretched over their hips, molding itself to their little tummys and pussys, which were clearly visible through the thin membrane. Next, Monique had them walk up to where we sat, turn around, and thrust out their little behinds, to show us the open network of their seats, the elastic strips stretched tautly across their young asses.

Now, wearing their black high heels and the tight-fitting rubber panties, they were marched to the punishment bars and made to assume the position.

Our three ex-gardeners now leaned over the top bar. Their high heels accented their straining calves as they stretched down to grasp the lower bar. They presented us with three pretty bottoms all in a row: Dawn's two firm rounded contours of smoothly tanned flesh, darkly split in the middle; Odette's, small, neat and perfectly rounded, with a deep tight fissure; and Heather's elongated swells of curv-

ing mounds, pulled taut by the pose and sep-
arated by a deep, amber arroyo.

I stole another glance at our guests. The
pretty assistant sat watching intently. Her
thighs were spread apart and her dress rucked
up to her waist. She was running her tongue
over her lips as her employer idly toyed with
her pussy, his eyes also fixed on the little
scene before us.

Because we were unsure of the strength of
their resolve to maintain their inverted positions, we thought it would be wise to secure
the girl's wrists to the lower bar, thereby assuring that they would keep their pose no
matter what. This Monique proceeded to do
tying wrist straps to the horseshoe-shaped staples set in the floor just beyond the bar. Their
ankles were left free so they could shift their
legs in response to the punishment.

Monique now was ready to demonstrate the
punishment panties. Stepping up to Dawn's
jutting ass, she grasped a single elastic strand
from the seat webbing between thumb and
forefinger, pulled it out about four inches,
and let go. It snapped back with a vicious
sting, hitting the spongy cheeks with a tiny
splat. We heard an "ouch" from the other
end of the inverted form.

Monique proceeded down the line, pluck-
ing the rubber bands and eliciting yelps, accompanied by tiny jerks as the elastic stung
their squirming behinds.

At this point Monique invited a little audience participation. Each of us stepped up to a

proferred ass. I selected the little blond's; our guest the soft hemispheres of Dawn; his assistant, the curving mounds of Heather. Then we joined in the fun. I plucked the elastic bands, stretching them to their outer limits, letting them snap back in rapid succession, punishing the cute round bottom. A series of red stripes appeared on the white flesh.

Reaching under her I tugged on the elastic at her crotch, and let it recoil with a splat into the tender pussyflesh. That time I got a loud yelp from my little victim. The sting must have smarted painfully as the rubber bit into the sensitive flesh of her hidden valley.

Now the three of us were totally engrossed in our work. The room filled with tiny yelps and squeals as rubber snapped against flesh. We were so absorbed we failed to notice the door open and a strange dark figure enter the room. Then, with a start, I turned to see a tall figure advancing on us. It was a female figure, covered from head to toe in black rubber. I recognized the mature, feminine curves immediately. It was Cora who had donned the rubber suit, and now intended to join in the festivities.

We stopped and stepped back, staring at the black form. The tight rubber hugged her body, moulding her curves like a second skin. Her breasts and her pointed nipples were clearly outlined; even the slight mound of her pubes stood out, clearly encased in the tight latex. She looked as though her body had been dipped in black paint.

* * *

With the full length body suit, Cora had donned rubber headgear which covered her head and face like a ski-mask, completely enclosing her blond hair in a tight fit around her head. She wore thin rubber gloves and, to complete her outfit, she wore long hip-length black boots, which moulded the sweeping contours of her long elegant legs.

Ritualistically, Monique gave the tall black figure a curt bow, and handed over her riding crop. Now the rubber-clad dominatrix strode up behind the shifting little bottoms, displayed so vulnerably before us. She took aim at the first, it was Dawn's, and sent a sharp sting cutting across the jiggling mounds. The young girl screamed at the top of her voice as the crop bit into her flesh with a resounding thwack.

With measured deliberation, Cora proceeded to the next victim, set her legs a little apart, and swung at the little blond's rear-end. Again a howl of pain shook the rafters. Then it was Heather's turn and equal treatment was meted out. Three times she repeated this, then she began to slash out indiscriminately. All three girls were yelling and sobbing as Cora lashed out in a frenzy, beating their red asses.

I looked around to find Mr. Seven. He had resumed his seat, and his little assistant was kneeling between his outstretched legs. She had his cock out and was ministering to his needs while he watched the erotic action under the lights.

*   *   *

When the spanking ended, Monique released the girls who, shaken and dazed, were allowed to rest before gathering up their clothes and leaving. Then Cora joined us, pulling off the rubber headgear. Her face was bathed in sweat; her hair soaked and disheveled. Her breath was labored, but her eyes shone with an eager gleam of intense passion. She was highly excited by the role she so loved to play.

As we were leaving Mr. Seven asked politely if he might have one of the brunettes sent to the guest's room which he shared with Miss Tai. Naturally, his wish was granted. She was of course, he added almost as an afterthought, to wear her rubber panties. We wholeheartedly agreed. For little Dawn this would be a night to remember.

CHAPTER SIX

Photo Opportunities

Once a year at Ironwood, a sort of graduation was held for those girls who had completed their training. These were young women who had had the word "no" banished from their lives, each inhibition systematically destroyed. Their sexual pleasure was now intimately bound up with their need to give pleasure to another, to serve. Such women, sure of their femininity, were in great demand by truly discriminating connoisseurs, as well as the owners of the most exclusive houses of pleasure on five continents.

In order to give each of our preferred clients an equal chance at employing our graduates, we held an annual auction. This event required as much preparation as the launching of a small war.

The first steps were taken months in advance, at which time work was begun on a catalogue of our current offerings, complete with color photos and relevant personal information on each of the girls. The Ironwood catalogues, printed in a limited edition, and carefully distributed to a select few, were eagerly sought after.

One of my duties at Ironwood was to supervise the production of this handsome volume, a task I did with considerable care and with loving attention to detail. Preparations began with an exclusive photo session for each of the girls. Since I was something of an amateur photographer, and since I knew most of the girls intimately, I decided to handle that assignment personally.

A large room was set aside as a studio, well-equipped with costumes and props. Day and evening sessions were scheduled to take advantage of the daylight and include both outdoor and indoor shots.

The first session had been scheduled with Kristen, a tall well-built blond, who was the healthy, outdoor type. I knew she loved horseback riding, and that seemed a good place to start. I arranged for her to meet me at the stable early one warm afternoon. She arrived dressed in her riding outfit: A crisp white blouse under a tailored charcoal blazer, matching jodhpurs, and a pair of polished black leather riding boots encasing her sturdy calves. Her long ash blond hair had been tucked up in a neat chignon, a few wispy strands escaping from under her black riding cap. Leather gloves and a short riding crop completed her outfit. Tall and elegant she cut a trim figure as she posed beside her favorite palamino for the first picture.

My plan was to pace her in one of the cars, taking a set of photos of the rider in various stages of undress. One of Cora's assistants was assigned to drive the car, and I climbed in beside her, my camera loaded and ready.

To start off I had the blond remove her jacket and blouse, baring a pair of medium sized tits capped with large fat nipples.

She started off at a trot, while I leaned out the window rapidly snapping pictures of the proud bare-breasted rider her ample tits bouncing delightfully in tempo with the trotting horse. Then she leaned forward, urging her mount to a gallop. Bending down, her breasts hung heavily under her, swaying rhythmically, the swollen tips brushing against the horse's mane, as she pounded along.

After a few minutes we stopped to arrange things for the next set to be taken after she had removed her pants. This took some doing as the snug boots had to be pulled off first, then the skin-tight riding pants. She squirmed and shimmied as she tugged the clinging pants over her hips and pulled them off her legs. Then she stood and placed her hands on her hips, and leaning forward with one quick motion slipped her panties down her legs. Then I had her put her boots back on.

She struck an alluring pose, her long torso totally naked from her cap to the tops of the shiny riding boots. Like all the girls of Ironwood, Kristen was perfectly at ease with her nudity. Unabashedly naked, she stood before me her hands on her hips, high-set breasts and pale triangle openly displayed, clutching her riding gloves and crop in her right hand.

As she re-mounted I stood behind her to get a shot of her lush bottom, and another one as she threw her leg over the horse opening her thighs to the eye of the camera.

Once again we took up our position behind the trotting horse and its bouncing rider. I had her stand in the stirrups to get some shots of her from behind; the even slope of her long back, the nicely-rounded buttocks, with athletic thighs and rigid legs holding herself proudly erect, as the horse raced across the meadow.

Finally, I wanted some shots of her alone, and for those we picked a leafy glade. A small overhang of rocks stood nearby bathed in the sun, a dramatic contrast against the shadows of the glade. Now the cap came off, and I had her release her hair from the knotted chignon. It fell to her naked shoulders in a pale silky mass. Her boots and gloves remained the sole items of clothing, as I helped her scramble up onto the rock formation (my helpful hand cupping her smooth ass as I boosted her up). She leaned back against the sun-splashed rocks, propped up on her elbows, and raising her knees, spreading them open as I posed her. Then, as the sunlight fell on her languid form, I had her insert the riding crop and gently, leisurely diddle herself for the camera.

The resulting picture was stunning. The horse grazed in the shadowy background, while in the foreground, bathed in golden sunlight, sprawled the lissome nude figure, her knees steepled, legs splayed open in loose abandon. One gloved hand gripped the thin black rod, buried halfway up her cunt. Her head was thrown back soft blond hair falling behind in a single silken sheath. Her eyes were half-lidded, and she wore an expression of dreamy repose in the quiet afternoon of that timeless place.

*   *   *

For Kristen's indoor shots she was mounted on a very different kind of horse. This scene took place in the punishment chamber deep in the basement of the manor house. The room was large and well-lit. The strong lights and stone walls gave it a stark appearance, although the deep-pile carpeting helped to soften things a bit. The room was furnished with hard benches, ladders, racks, trestles, and various other instruments of punishment. Most of the devices looked a lot more threatening than they actually were. Still the room was regarded with dread by those hapless females who knew of the bizarre punishments which awaited them there.

Kristen's mount this time was a sturdy trestle, padded, and covered with leather. A girl, mounting the "horse," used a small step and swung one leg over, then very carefully, eased herself down. Her caution was understandable for mounted on the center of the crossbar was a hard rubber dildo onto which she had to lower herself.

Once again I had Kristen dressed, or rather undressed, as she had been that afternoon, naked but for her riding accouterments: cap, gloves and boots. I helped her mount up, watching intrigued as she carefully straddled the trestle, her hands on the crossbar, supporting her weight as she gingerly lowered herself while the greased pole disappeared up her yawning cunt.

I took a few quick shots as she impaled herself on the fake cock, a look of apprehension on her pretty features as she settled into place. Next using the steps placed under each booted foot I had her raise and lower herself several times, fucking herself on the stiff rod. Her hands on her hips, her powerful legs bent in a squat and then straightened rigidly. After several minutes of this lewd exercise, the camera clicking constantly, the blond rider was breathing heavy, her face flushed and mouth open. I kept her at it till she finished herself off, capturing the orgasmic sequence on film.

*   *   *

The next session on my schedule was Jacqueline's. Jackie was an old acquaintance whom I had known since my first days at Ironwood. Even now, although she was all of eighteen years old, I still thought of her as I had first seen her, a pubescent blond doing her dance exercises in the nude, one day long ago.

Slim-hipped with a lithe narrow figure and a look of childish innocence, Jackie had retained a decidedly girlish quality. And so I decided to show her as a young girl. Accordingly we went to the "playground," a sandy pit with swings, and slides and such, now rarely used, far behind the main house. She had dressed as I ordered, face freshly scrubbed, blond hair pulled back neatly in a pony-tail, and a little girl's dress with short puffy sleeves, a lacy collar, and a stiff skirt which stood out and barely covered her behind, provided she didn't bend over. The bodice of the dress flattened her nascent breasts. Thin white cotton socks and a pair of patent leather shoes completed the outfit. At my instructions she had worn no panties.

I had her pose for me, climbing the steps of the sliding board as I crawled under her, pointing the camera up at her bare behind. I caught her in mid-step, one foot up, the other lower, spreading her little pussy. As she climbed above me I had her reach back, raise her dress, and jut out her bottom invitingly. I got some superb shots of her tight young behind, white and smooth, and neatly bisected by a thin dark centercrease. From underneath the ladder the camera saw all, the vulnerable pussy half open, with its pale haze of sparse blond fuzz.

I had a special effect in mind for the seesaw. At one end I affixed a thin black rubber dildo, strapping its base to the board. My next series of shots had the "little girl" curiously examining the stiff rod. Then, with some experimentation, she straddled the board, easing herself down onto the dildo. I worked the other end, pushing it down, giving her a ride of bouncing erotic thrills. As she was propelled upwards, her eyebrows shot up, eyes widening in surprised delight at the novel sensation. While she rode the dildo, I was busy snapping off shots from in front, behind, and under the bouncing adolescent.

Now I posed her on the swings, sliding back to sit on her thighs, her ass hanging out in the back as I lay behind her, and with a little shove, got her swinging up and over me and the prying camera. Finally, I had her bend over as if to tie her shoe. Naturally the little dress rode up revealing her bare asscheeks. She turned to look behind her at the camera, a cute look of shocked innocence on her pretty face.

My afternoon session with the "little girl" was getting me eager to do something more than take pictures. It was fucking time. And so we ended the session with me laying on my back in the sandpit, the girl in the little party dress, straddling me, her bare bottom inches from my face as she squatted down on my straining cock. The camera lay at one side, temporarily forgotten.

For the evening session I wanted to contrast the "little girl" quality of Jackie, with the sophisticated lady named Jacqueline. For this

purpose I had several evening gowns, modi-
fied to my specifications, in which I intended
to dress her.

She arrived for the session looking every
bit the statuesque blond, a picture of chic
sophistication. Her hair had been set in an
elegant coiffeur. She was exquisitely made
up: her wide blue eyes lined with radiant
ultramarine, a touch of blush applied to her
high cheekbones. The dark vermillion on her
lush lips gave them a wet and gleaming look.
She had donned a pair of sparkling pendant
earrings; a high rhinestone choker encircled
her pretty neck.

The first outfit I had chosen for her was an
elegant narrow sheath of jet black satin. It
tightly clung to her curves behind, and a slit
up the side exposed a length of dark nylon
stocking. But the most distinguished feature
of the gown was the low cut in front. In fact it
was so low that it left the wearer's breasts
exposed. Two thin black straps X-ed across
her chest crossing just below her small sexy
boobs.

To maintain the atmosphere of elegance, I
scheduled this session for the dining room,
the table having been set with fine silver, and
the soft glow of candles providing the lighting. I had my pretty model pose, a glass of
wine to her lips, while I took closeup shots of
her adorable face, long neck and swaying
maidenly breasts. She had applied just a hint
of color to her nipples, and they gleamed in

the candlelight, which bathed her soft flesh in a golden glow.

With some reluctance I had to shatter this mood to change my film and get my model to change her dress. The second outfit was also a straight sheath, this one made of clinging silvery silk. With it she wore pale silvery nylons held in place by a thin garter belt. The gown had a deep scoop-neck which allowed a generous view of her little breasts, but the most dramatic feature of this gown was apparent in the view from behind.

In the back a rectangular panel had been cut out from the waist down and about eighteen inches wide. The effect was to expose her rearmounds and the backs of her long nyloned legs. From behind the camera caressed her elegant contours from her bare ass down her taut thighs and all the way to her delicate stiletto shoes which, keeping her high on her toes, shaped her calves in slim elongated curves. She was a dazzling sight.

For this part of the session, I had set up some powerful lights on the roof and we proceeded there now. The manor house had a small turret on one front corner, and it was there that I decided to pose my model. We started up the circular staircase, she in front, and I just behind, watching the shifting of her firm buttocks inches from my face as we climbed the steep stairs.

I posed her leaning over the parapet as if lost in a dream. From behind the pose stretched her taut leg muscles which, encased in silvery nylon, set off dramatically the dazzling white flesh of her naked thighs and bottom. As she leaned forward her ass peeked out of the back of the dress, the sweet rounded contours shifting in erotic invitation.

Finally, I had her turn around and face one of the stone walls on the inside of the turret, pressing her chest to the wall, spreading her legs as far as the tight dress would allow, and reaching with her hands for the stars. The silvery dress and white flesh contrasted dramatically with the dark grey stones. In this stretched position, her ass once more bared to the camera, I found her irresistible. Quietly, I laid the camera down and approached her from behind, sliding my hands around her to grasp her silken breasts. Then we were on the roof, with her once again straddling me, the slink fabric rucked up to her waist. She writhed, grinding her hips down onto me, and keening in wild passion.

*   *   *

The next girl to report for a photo session was Arianne, a rather thin leggy girl with short straight auburn hair. I had arranged it that we would meet at the large indoor pool near the gymnasium. Since the girls always swam in the nude, there was no need to specify an outfit for the occasion.

I studied her naked body with the eye of a professional photographer. She had an alert, lively face, curious eyes, and a small upturned nose. Her shoulders were rather too thin, and angular, and her breasts were modest feminine beginnings. Narrow and pointy they ended in cocoa brown tips. Below her tits her slim lines flowed into a slight indentation at her belly which formed a concave hollow between her prominent hipbones. Her sex was marked by a thick riot of tiny brown coils sprinkled over the narrow triangle of her neat vulva. Her legs were straight and muscular, with a slight feminine curve to her thighs.

Arianne was an expert swimmer and diver. I had her mount the divingboard now, and pose at the ready position, legs tight together, arms at her side, standing on the end of the board. I got a few shots from behind of the tall thin figure with the tight young ass. Then I had her do a set of dives as I snapped from the poolside. She did a series of long graceful dives, her arms extended, her body arched as she cut through the air, naked and free.

I waited to catch her as she emerged from the pool, climbing the ladder with water streaming off of her supple body. Then I took off my clothes and joined her in the pool, my camera protected by its underwater case. Now I took another shot of her going up the ladder, this time from underwater. Her little round ass glowed in the bluish-green light, as I squeezed off another shot. Then I had her swim underwater for the camera, capturing her slow dream-like movements, legs and arms twining as she slowly tumbled and twisted underwater. I spent another roll of film recording that fascinating underwater ballet.

*   *   *

The night scenes for Arianne had been scheduled for the punishment chamber. Because her limbs were so long and thin, I felt it might be interesting to see her stretched to her limits. For this purpose I intended to display Arianne on the X-frame. This was a cross made of two boards with large iron staples fixed at the four extremes.

First, thick black straps were buckled around the girl's wrists and ankles. These leather cuffs had D-rings attached to them, so that a rope or chain could be conveniently attached. Then the girl was backed up against the crossed boards, her arms extended up and out, legs outstretched. I backed Arianne into that position now, her tanned body highlighted by the leather bands and the high heels, which were her only articles of clothing. Next, I attached a rope to each cuff, pulling the line taut, stretching her tightly against the board. The position wasn't exactly painful, but it was uncomfortable, and it left the girl totally open to one's gaze, or the camera's eye.

I let the camera lovingly explore the long lines, the straining muscles of calves and thighs, the graceful curves of that long lissome body, and the slender outstretched arms. Because her arms were pulled out and a little back, the elongated swells of her tits were somewhat flattened by the pose, melding into her soft supple chest. But her pointy nipples remained darkly prominent. Hard and swollen now, they were stiff with the first hint of feminine arousal.

Her pussy, pulled open by the spread-leg position, was a glistening pink slit, the lips slightly distended and swollen, set deep in a tangle of soft springy curls. I couldn't resist sticking a finger in there. She was very wet. It was obvious that posing for me was exciting her.

The last pose I selected for the delectable Arianne would also take advantage of her tall willowy frame. For this I removed her from the crossboards and placed her underneath a hook which hung from a ceiling rafter in this well-equipped room. Tying her wrists together, I attached them to the hook. Next, I applied a spreader bar to her ankles, forcing them apart about three feet, as her ankle straps were clipped to each end of the bar. Finally, I hauled on the other end of the rope, which ran over a pulley placed just above the rafter.

With a few pulls I had her dangling in the air, six inches or so off the floor. She moaned a little at the strain on her arms. I knew the position would hurt, but I only intended to leave her like that long enough to satisfy the demands of the camera.

I took a series of shots of the hanging brunette her pussy spread open invitingly. I photographed her from behind, from in front, and laying down on the floor, from underneath, shooting up at her vulnerable pussy. For the last shots I removed the spreader bar. Now her willowy frame hung in long graceful lines from the wrists high over her head, to her little toes, curled and straining just a few inches from the floor, as her body swayed slightly suspended in the air.

*   *   *

The next girl selected for a photo session was Nichole. With her long black hair and willowy pale body, she was at her most erotic, her pale flesh was banded with black leather. The contrast of the primitive image of a female in bondage with the trappings of refined civilization, intrigued me, and so I arranged to have Nichole meet me in the library.

The room was richly paneled in dark stained oak. It contained a large collection of hand-tooled leather bound volumes devoted largely to erotica, providing a convenient reference source for the instructional efforts at Ironwood. Large folios of erotic photos, drawings, and paintings were also available for the perusal of residents and guests. As for the rest, the room contained a number of sturdy oak tables, and deep, comfortable Morris chairs of well-worn leather. Daylight filtered in through narrow cut glass windows, providing a soft light for my photographic study.

I was setting up my equipment when there was a knock at the door. Nichole entered dressed in the pearl grey tunic she seemed to prefer, her head lowered, her falling hair draping her face.

"Strip Nikkie," I ordered casually. "Down to your panties."

While Nichole shed her clothes, I turned my back on her to fiddle with the camera. When I turned around she was ready, her long white body gloriously naked from the soft flowing hair down to her pretty delicate feet. Except for the skimpy panties slung low on her hips, her lissome lines were smooth and unbroken.

Now I took up a series of straps which I had brought from the punishment cell. I began by cuffing her wrists with wide wrist-bands. Then pulling her arms behind her, I snapped the cuffs together with a spring clip binding her wrists behind her back.

The next set of straps went around her upper arms. I circled them tightly, the leather indenting the soft flesh. These too were clipped together, the effect being to pull back her shoulders, thrusting her high-set breasts proudly forward. Broader, thicker straps were placed midway up each thigh. Again I cinched them tightly, the leather digging into the soft flesh. These straps were joined together by a short lead, which hobbled her movements.

Next I placed a broad belt just above her hips, pulling it tightly as possible so as to constrict her narrow waist even more. The last set of straps were ankle cuffs. As a final touch I affixed a collar around her pretty neck. This was a band about four inches wide with a convenient D-ring, useful should it be necessary to place her on a leash.

With the straps securely in place, I was ready to start shooting. First I helped her to one of the Morris chairs. I had her kneel on the seat, facing the back of the chair, and tilted forward so that her chest, just above the breasts, rested on the back of the chair. Her pale twin hemispheres jutted back saucily, framed between the belt at her waist and the thick straps encircling her thighs.

For the next series of shots I used a large round hassock. I released her wrists and arms, leaving the straps in place. Then, turning the squat cylinder on its side and rolling it a little forward, I had her sprawl backwards on it. Now her supple figure was bent over backwards, her back supported by the hassock, her love mound thrust forward, lasciviously aimed straight at the camera. Her head lolled back, her hair falling in a sweeping fan to the carpet below. I nudged her legs open. Her muscles strained to hold the position, her pussy slit spread open. The dark pink of the inner flesh of the ragged lips clearly visible in the nest of tiny black curls. She held the pose, exposing her glistening cunt to the all-seeing camera's eye, as I snapped merrily away.

Next, I placed her on her knees, her forehead touching the floor in submissive bondage. The pose highlighted her naked haunches, and the lovely swells of her upturned bottom.

Once again I was finding it difficult to concentrate on my work. This bound woman was getting to me. As I looked at her in the love slave's position, patiently holding the pose I had ordered, I had a strong urge to take

advantage of the lewd invitation offered by
her jutting behind.

I had her stand up and come around to the
back of the chair. Then I made her drape her
supple form over the back. Clasping her
around the wrists I pulled her arms down,
stretching them down the sides, and tying the
cuffs to the arms of the chair. Now standing
behind her, I spread her ankles tying one to
each leg of the chair. Controlling my impulse
to lay into her, I took a few more pictures
from behind first, her legs stretched taut, the
rounded swells of her ass upturned in offering.

From the front the camera caught a mouth-
watering view of her hanging tits swaying between tautly stretched arms. I couldn't resist
reaching up to tweak a nipple. Rolling the
nub between thumb and forefinger, I felt the
tip stiffen in response. Nichole was the kind
of woman who liked showing her body and
she became easily aroused by the slightest
display.

Now, stepping behind her, I set the camera
down, and slowly dropped my pants, slipping
my briefs down in one easy motion. I then
knelt down behind the bent form, my face
just inches from her pussy. I studied her tight
cheeks, the rounded bottoms curving in to
the soft underfolds of her pussy, the sprinkling of soft springy hairs trailing through
the valley between the sculpted contours of
her taut rounded thighs.

I strained upward bringing my lips nearer
and lightly slid my tongue along the groove.

Nichole sighed deeply and twitched at the sudden intimate tickling. My face and nose pressed tight against the soft folds of her pussy. I licked along the ridge straining to reach the hot wet cavern. From somewhere far away I heard a moan, muffled by the silken thighs clamped against my ears.

I backed out a little, and ran my tongue along the soft undercurves of each cheek. This brought another moan and a plaintive cry for more as she writhed sensuously in response to my thorough licking of her ass. Next, I paused to plant a kiss on each perfect cheek, letting lips and tongue trace a wet trail up over the smooth silky mounds.

Next, stiffening my tongue, I inserted it into the deep amber crease between her clenching cheeks. Nichole whimpered pleadingly. Slowly I ran it up and down the crack, the bound girl emitting a series of deep throated "ahhhs," with each lick. She was wriggling her ass now as the fragrance of a female in heat permeated the air. I palmed her love pouch, savoring the fragrant moisture, the damp heat, of burgeoning arousal radiating from her cunt.

Now I placed a hand on each cheek, pressing my thumbs into her crack to pry her open for a good look at her tiny brown asshole. I began licking at her hidden rose, flicking my tongue and stabbing at that secret place. She jerked in her bonds with a mighty heave, a cry of passion escaped her lips. I stabbed at the little hole again and again. A shudder ran through her body and she cried out:

"Oh, fuck me, fuck me, fuck me . . . please fuck me," she pleaded, tossing her head from side to side, caught up in her passion.

Standing up, I lubricated my stiff rod with saliva, and stepped up against her lovely swells to insert my prick in the thin shadow crease between the mounds. I let it rest there a moment, content to luxuriate in the feel of the moist heat as the silken strip of innerflesh caressed my rock-hard prick.

Then I placed the tip against the tight ring of rubbery flesh and pressed, forcing the gate, impaling her on my rigid cock. I shoved in a few more inches. She grunted and mumbled incoherently. Now I was buried all the way up her hot little rectum, pressing my hips against the warm pliant swells.

I reached around her sleek sides to grab onto her swaying tits. As I clutched those narrow tit-bags, Nicole wiggled her ass happily, thrusting back against me, demanding more.

Then I was fucking her ass, sawing in and out with long deep thrusts. Her hot tight asshole yielding and clutching at my cock as we mounted the heights of passion. Now the demented girl was babbling incoherently, straining to shove her ass back at me, writhing in a frenzy of uncontrollable passion and pleading for more, and more, and more.

At last I felt her body begin to shake, a slight tremor growing into a series of strong spasms which shook her slight frame. Suddenly she tightened on me, her body rigid, her ass clenching my cock spasmodically. I lost all control plunging furiously into her with one brutal thrust, burying my rod to the hilt, spurting jets of cum straight up her hot little ass.

We groaned together and I fell forward, laying my head on the smooth slope of her warm moist back, and gasping for air. Nichole was sobbing uncontrollably as tiny aftershocks coursed through her body. We stayed in that position, her bent over and tethered, me too spent to move, exhausted, draped over her bent form, as the waves of pleasure subsided into a warm afterglow.

CHAPTER SEVEN

Private Lessons

The seasons seemed to change more slowly at Ironwood. It was a clear, sharp September day. The tall oaks overarching the driveway were resplendent in their fall colors: fiery reds, blazing oranges, and vibrant yellows. I had just returned from the deserts of Arabia, and the cool crispness in the air seemed a blessing to me.

Monique met me at the door to inform me that Cora had gone to London to make some arrangements for a group of new arrivals. My guest room had been prepared for me, and Cora had left instructions to see to it that I was provided with suitable entertainment in the persons of Marilee and Odette, two of our young charges who, she added with a leering grin, might need some guidance from time to time. I generously allowed as how I was willing to work with the less experienced girls as part of my responsibilities to Ironwood.

Monique asked if there was anything else; any special needs or desires I might have for the evening. I told her that as a matter of fact there was one small thing, and I wished to have it delivered to my room immediately.

After dinner that night, I took a stroll. I lingered in the garden, drinking in the bracing night air. As I wandered back to my room, I made a detour through the darkened kitchen to pick up a few things that I thought would come in handy.

My room remained unchanged from my last stay, except for the large air mattress which Monique had installed at my request. It had been set conveniently between the bed and the bathroom.

I slowly stripped and turned on the bathtub taps, filling the tub with hot sudsy water. Then I emersed myself in the soft warmth, for a long leisurely soak. I was toweling myself off when I heard a hesitant rapping at my bedroom door. Still in the nude, I padded over to throw back the door. There stood two delectable female creatures dressed in the tunics and short skirts of Ironwood, complete with nylons and high heels. They reminded me of two little girls dressed up and trying so hard to look like ladies.

Marilee's outfit was a soft cream color with buff-colored nylons; Odette was dressed all in a deep dark blue, her shiny opaque nylons were a vibrant electric blue, and she wore shoes to match. They looked up at me in wide-eyed surprise, running their eyes quickly down the front of my body, and shyly bowing their little heads. Not a word was spoken as I stepped back and ushered them into the room.

I had the apprehensive duo wait beside my bed while I lay back, propped up on the pillows. I told them they were to take off their shoes and strip to their underwear and nylons. When that was done, I had them kneel in the Ironwood position females assumed in presenting themselves to the male: sitting back on their heels, thighs spread open, arms at the side, palms open and facing front. My little charges assumed the familiar pose, their heads bent submissively, their eyes averted as they had been taught.

I kept them waiting there, on their knees, for quite a while, before ordering the removal of their bras. They reached back to undo the clasps, shrugging slim shoulders and brushing the flimsy straps down slender arms, as they freed their young, adolescent breasts.

Marilee's were small, but round and fully-formed. About the size of ripe plums, they were crowned with two dark brown disks, the pert little nipples pointing slightly up and outward. They were miniature versions of the fuller mounds of a mature woman. Odette's still-budding breasts also showed the promise of womanhood. Two tiny pale brown nipples marked the slight swells on her nubile torso. I studied the top of her bowed head as she knelt there. Her long blond hair, tied back in a ponytail, was soft and shiny.

I decided that the panties must go next, a

task I relished. Swinging my legs over the bed so I could sit on the edge, I had Marilee stand and come over to me. I beckoned her even closer, to get her within reach between my legs. Then, I had her put her hands on the back of her head, the pose causing her little boobs to stretch and stir.

Next I reached out for her running my hands down her smooth flanks and onto the ridge of lacy elastic at her hips. Slipping my fingers into the waistband at each side I slowly lowered the creamy nylon barrier over the even smoothness of her belly to reveal a small, plump love purse, sprinkled with a dusting of sandy curls. I grabbed the nylon by the crotch and yanked it over her thighs and down her legs. She hopped a little as she stepped free of the crumpled panties now ringing her ankles.

I wanted a close-up view of her little pussy. Placing a hand on each hip, I pulled her towards me.

"Spread your legs a little," I whispered hoarsely. My throat had gone suddenly dry. Obediently, she shifted, opening her stance. With fingers still hooked behind her head, she stared straight ahead not daring to look down without my permission. I gazed at the dusky pink slit just a few inches from my eyes, but I resisted the urge to reach out and touch her. Instead I pulled her by the hips, bringing her sex closer and lowering my head to sample her sexual aroma. Inhaling deeply, I caught a whiff of her delicate tangy smell, a hint of feminine arousal, slightly fishy, reminiscent of the sea.

"Now you can drop your hands. Put them on your pussy. Open it up. I want you to show me the inside."

Opening her legs even further apart and squatting a little, she reached down, her fingers entering her cunt, from both sides. Then she pried the fleshy gates aside, revealing the smooth inner recesses of her sex. In a moment I released her, and had her resume her place on her knees.

Next, I beckoned the shy Odette to me. She approached cautiously, with a little tentative smile. I let my eyes drink in her lithe body, the slim hips, slender thighs, girlish arms and legs, and budding breasts. The little bumps shifted temptingly when she stretched up to link her hands behind her head.

I reached out to her slight waist, resting my hands for a moment on her trim hips, then, without further ado, I stripped off her skimpy panties, slipping the shiny blue veil over the flare of her cradling hips. The silky garment clung to her crotch for a moment, caught up in the damp crevice. Reaching between her legs, I plucked it free. The wispy material tumbled down her straight, girlishly-attractive legs to ring her ankles.

The unveiling exposed the small mound of her pubes with its neat centertuck, and just the merest trace of pussyhair. Pale and blond, her triangle was nicely framed by the thin blue elastic bands of the garter belt. My hands curled easily around her neat hips, my fingers digging into her pliant asscheeks, as I hauled her forward, bringing her pussy closer. Glancing up to see her reaction to this intimate inspection, I was startled to find her staring down at me, her blue eyes wide with intense interest.

I brought a hand up between her young thighs, and saw just the slightest quiver ripple through her belly in anticipation of my intimate touch. But I didn't touch her love pouch, at least not just then, preferring for the moment to just tease, grazing the thin veneer of wispy pussyfur, brushing the pads of my fingertips lightly up and down her soft blond fuzz.

"Use your fingers to open yourself up. Show me," I mumbled.

The girl shifted her stance, spreading her nylon-clad legs, and squatting slightly, so that she could open her crotch. Then she reached down and pried apart the fleshy netherlips, holding herself open with her splayed fingers, wantonly showing her pale pink flower. Glancing up, I found the girl had her eyes closed, her lips curled and pressed tightly together. Her slight breasts gently rose and fell to her shallow even breathing.

I released her and had her resume her place on her knees beside her sister. Now I gave my charges a lecture on auto-eroticism and the joys of masturbation. I offered to instruct them in some of the finer points. For demonstration purposes, we would start with some common household objects. I had them place two chairs beside the bed, sit down and scoot their bottoms forward. I then arranged them the way I wanted them, their knees steepled, legs folded back, thighs spread. Grabbing a hold of their stockinged legs by the ankles, I draped them over each arm of the chair. They sat there, as I posed them, pussys shamelessly exposed, while I rummaged through the cabinets for a box of candles. I came back with two solid wax tapers, each about ten inches long.

Handing one to each girl, I told them that I wanted to see their techniques. They knew what to do. Without hesitation, they inserted the hard wax rods, Marilee with casual nonchalance that suggested she had had some practice; Odette more tentatively, using one hand to open her lips and cautiously inserting the narrow end of the waxen shaft with the other. Impatiently, I urged them on. Getting a firm grip on their candles, the girls began a pumping motion, moving their little fists up and down, plunging and extracting the waxen rods with concentrated effort.

"Faster!" I hissed.

At my whispered command the action became more heated, the little fists pistoning up and down furiously. Both girls had closed their eyes. Marilee's head lolled backwards; her mouth fell open; her tongue peeked out to slowly sensuously rim her lips. Odette's pretty face was screwed up in inner concentration, her eyes clamped shut as she beat off with intense determination, her upper body straining against the chair. Both girls were making urgent little sounds now, their cries rising in intensity. But I didn't want them to come, not just yet. So I stopped them.

"Enough," I commanded.

Marilee whimpered a little in frustration. Puffing like an overworked steam engine, her labored breathing gradually subsided. Odette, her eyes still closed, seemed to shiver as her breathing settled down. I had them shove the candles in as far as they would go, lodging them firmly up their cunts, the white ends peeking out obscenely. As they sat there, legs spread, cunts stuffed, I told them about the second lesson that I had planned.

I opened the package I had carried from the kitchen, and extracted two cucumbers. Long and bulky, these sturdy vegetables would provide a cunt-full for my little girls. I had them remove the candles and scramble up onto the bed. Meanwhile I opened a bottle of vegetable oil and proceeded to oil up the green dildoes.

I explained that while girls could give pleasure to themselves using common household objects, they could also use such humble means for pleasuring a friend. As I spoke I arranged my nymphets the way I wanted them, head to tail. Marilee lay on her side, her bottom leg foreward and bent slightly to provide a pillow for the little blond who rested her head on that thigh. In this way, each had ready access to the other's cunt, a few inches from her face. I handed each a greasy cucumber, and told them to go at it.

The little brunette lifted a leg to allow easier entry, while Odette spread hers to make things easier for her friend's probing fingers. Then the sturdy vegetables were cautiously inserted and slowly worked up and down as the girls tested their limits to accommodate.

Since the pair had been well-aroused by the preceding session with the candles, it didn't take much stimulation to raise them back to a fevored pitch. I watched the shiny vegetables plunging in and out, stretching their cuntlips. The dildoes were glistening with their sexjuices, and they were emitting tiny moans of passion, as they worked over one another energetically. Soon their moans were becoming more insistent, louder, more urgent; hips and thighs churning and bucking uncontrollably, they were swept up in their onrushing orgasms. Marilee, thrashing about wildly, came with a toss of her head and a scream of passion; Odette clamped her thighs together on the sturdy vegetable, her thin reedy body stiffening, and let out a thin whimper through tightly-pressed lips. Then her thighs slackened and her legs loosely fell apart.

* * *

I let them rest awhile, while I prepared the third demonstration. For this lesson, I had secured two long thin carrots from the kitchen, which I now proceeded to oil. Once again, some re-arranging was called for. This time I stretched out first, in the middle of the bed, placing a playmate on either side, with their heads towards the foot of the bed. Then I had them turn over on their bellys, shoving pillows under their hips, and spreading their nylon-clad legs a little.

The effect was to elevate their cute rounded bottoms most invitingly. The cucumbers, still lodged in their cunts, protruded lewdly from between their legs. Then I was explaining that there was still another way to have fun with the common garden variety vegetable. I moved down on the bed until I was between the two uplifted bottoms, my carrots at the ready.

I first attended to Odette, whose ass lay under my right hand. Spanning a hand across both small mounds, I squeezed them together, fondling and caressing them. Her young ass was perfect: pale, soft, pliant and satiny smooth. Reaching over I placed the splayed fingers of my left hand firmly across her centercrease, and pressing down I spread her cheeks apart, opening the dark shadowline between her rubbery pillows, to reveal the pale pink bud of her anus.

Very carefully, I introduced the tapered end of the carrot to the puckered dimple. Slowly but relentlessly, I pressed against the tiny gate until it yielded and the tip squeezed in. Giving her time to accommodate, I waited while the small ring of muscle contracted spasmodically, the sides of her buttocks hollowing as her cheeks clenched reflexively. In a moment her muscles slackened and I drove the shaft in another inch or so. Once a few inches were up her behind, I stopped, letting her get used to the idea of having the carrot up her ass, while I turned to her girlfriend.

Once again I began by feeling up her lovely young ass, massaging the delectable behind that was offered so temptingly to my left hand. I smacked her playfully just to see her cheeks clench in surprised reaction. The rounded domes of her asscheeks were incredibly smooth and silky to the touch. I let my fingers linger over those lush orbs, tracing little circles on each mound. Finally, I opened her tight cheeks peering into the shadowy crack at her asshole, pinkish brown and crinkly. The rubbery ring contracted spasmodically as I placed a fingertip on her brown rose and pushed.

Now, holding the pliant rubbers apart with one hand, I placed the tip of the carrot just at the tiny orifice. I thought to plunge it all the way in, in one penetrating drive, but resisted the temptation. Instead I used short, relentless jabs, working the carrot up her ass with the impaled girl grunting, deep throaty grunts, with each tiny thrust. Gradually, her resistance slackened and she accepted more and more of it. Both girls now had two or three inches of carrot up their ass, with several inches sticking out behind.

Firmly gripping each carrot I diddled their little assholes, drilling into them, turning the sturdy stalks and pressing in, then jiggling them in and out. In a little while I had them squirming their hips, bouncing and humping up and down vigorously in response to my manipulations. Wriggling, flopping, and thrashing about, both girls were on their sides now, their hands clutching the cucumbers still embedded in their cunts. I let them fuck themselves as I diddled their asses. In this way the frenzied females were driven towards their second shattering climax of the night.

Naturally, all these erotic games were having an effect on me. I had had a hardon since my two nymphets had taken off their bras. It seemed as if I had been stiff for hours. My cock was throbbing with impatience to lay into these young, nubile bodies.

Eagerly, I got both girls to sit up and remove their nylons and garter belts. Now, completely naked, the three of us climbed on the rubber mattress. I grabbed a bottle of body oil; poured myself a generous handful, and slapped it onto Marilee's soft little chest. Handing the bottle to Odette, I had her oil herself all over. Meanwhile I ran my slippery hands over Marilee's emerging feminine curves, down her long smooth legs, up the calves in back, and onto her ass.

When both female bodies were gleaming with a sheen of oil, I layed down on my side. Odette I placed on her side in front of me, my cock just touching her ass. I reached around to grab her slippery boobs and pulled her back against me, my stiff cock nestled in the warm tight valley between her cheeks. Marilee I had get behind me and drape her body over mine, pressing her warm tits into

my back, her love-mound rubbing against my
ass. Then I had them move. Squirming and
grinding against slippery female flesh I rock-
eted off to a pounding climax, spurting my
cum in throbbing spasms, splattering Odette's
young bottom with gobs of thick cream.

*   *   *

Sometime later that night I got ready to
take charge at the evening's punishment call.
Usually this was duty that Cora saw to personally, but in her absence, I had volunteered
to conduct the session. I had asked Victor,
who had been staying at Ironwood that weekend, to accompany me. Victor, I knew, had a
lively imagination and always enjoyed meting
out a little discipline to a deserving female.
We arranged to meet in the punishment chamber later that evening.

In accordance with the protocol laid down
for this ritual, the miscreants, usually charged
with violating one of Ironwood's many rules
and regulations, were ordered to present themselves for punishment at the appointed time
wearing stripped to their underwear and stockings. Thus upon entering the cell, they were
immediately reminded of their vulnerability.
Cora inevitably dressed in black in her role as
disciplinarian. I had what I hoped was an
appropriate outfit: boots, riding pants, and a
loose leather vest, over my bare chest. Victor,
dressed a little more conservatively, wore plain
dark trousers and a white silk shirt, which he
left casually open down the front.

Our victim, there was only one that night,

was a tall elegant blond named Ashley. The girls who passed through Ironwood came from a wide variety of backgrounds, but seldom did we get someone like Ashley. She was nineteen, proud and aristocratic, from a wealthy family. A pampered, snobbish, daughter who enjoyed all the privileges of wealth. She had also had an obsessive need to be debased, subjugated, and humiliated. For her, sexual pleasure was inexorably bound up with submission. The lower the degradation, the higher were the peaks of ecstatic pleasure.

She found her way to Ironwood, a bored, blase, rich girl, seeking the ultimate sexual experience; seeking someone to do what no one had ever been able to do, totally dominate her. She was taken in reluctantly, for Cora seldom accepted girls that old as novices. Still she had been so persistent, she had been allowed to stay. She was constantly breaking rules, and constantly being punished.

Tonight she stood submissively before us clad in nothing but a black bra and panties, with sleek smoky-tinted nylons. The contrast with her pale beauty was striking. Ashley had silvery blond hair, long and straight, falling in a silken mantle to caress her slim shoulders. She had chisled features with the high cheekbones of a fashion model, a long aristocratic nose, and searching eyes, blue-gray eyes, seductive, distant and vaguely disquieting. Her mouth was wide and sensuous, but serious. I never saw her smile. Now she stood before us awaiting her sentence, her head lowered, hands loosely at her side, stockinged feet spread a little apart.

Immediately, we had her remove her brassiere. She sloughed off the lacy black garment, uncovering a lovely pair of breasts, firm, uptilted cones, slightly flattened and set high on her lithe torso. Her mouth-watering nipples were large and pink, the little nubs, protruding out, already stiff and distended in anticipation of what we might do to her.

We intended to start by displaying Ashley's tall blond body on the rack. Actually, the rack was a padded leather table with a cylindrical drum at its head. Ashley knew the routine. We watched her scramble up onto the padded tabletop, treating us to a view of her superb ass tightly packed in black satiny nylon. She arranged herself on her back, her legs spread, hands together and stretched up over her head.

We cuffed her wrists with wide leather straps, the cuffs linked together and attached to a rope extending from the drum over her head. Similar cuffs were clamped on her slim ankles and attached to ropes running to anchors set at each corner of the table. Those lines were pulled taut, stretching the nylon-clad legs; the strain evident in the taut muscles of her tapering thighs.

Now Victor walked to the crank at the side of the drum and gave it a half turn. The slack was taken up and the girl's arms were pulled upward over her head. Victor cranked in several more notches until her long slender arms were fully extended, the sleek lines pulled taut from wrists to shoulders. One more notch was taken up, and the wheel locked in place. We didn't go further because our purpose was not to hurt her, but rather to place her in a helpless position one in which she would be maximally exposed, open to whatever we chose to do to her defenseless body.

She made a breathtaking picture stretched out on the table. The sinews of her long arms took much of the strain, the soft underarms showing just a trace of blond stubble, the taut body with streamlined curves sweeping down to flaring hips; narrow, elongated thighs framed by the black lacy straps of the garter belt and dramatically set off by the dark top bands of the nylons tightly encasing her long dancer's legs.

Her breasts, somewhat flattened by her stretched position, were distended into two gentle swells, but her upstanding nipples stood at attention, proud and erect, blatent evidence of her aroused state. As of yet her sex had remained covered by the skimpy black panties, slung low across her cradling hips. That would change very soon, but for now we would leave her to herself, to contemplate her fate, while Victor and I had a cigarette, and laid our plans for her.

We decided to test her responsiveness to stimulation. For that we wanted her completely naked. We each took an ankle, untied her and removed the leather bands. Ashley lay there as though asleep, totally unresponsive, her eyes closed, limbs slack, acquiescent to whatever manner we chose to arrange her splendid body. When it came time for her panties, Victor gallantly insisted that I do the honors.

My hands trembled in eagerness as I placed at each side, my thumbs on her hipbones. Then, spanning her slim waist with my hands, I worked the little garment over the angular hipbones, and down the slight indentation of her belly, and on down the smooth flow of her tapered thighs, unveiling the slight mound of her sex with its sliver gold fleece. The soft curlings began as a sparse row at the top edge of the triangle, thickening into a cloudy tuft at the apex, and trailing down between her loosely-parted legs. I brushed my fingers through the silken fleece and then palmed her crotch, testing her, and getting a deep sigh in response. She was slightly moist but not yet wet between the legs. Impatiently, I yanked the flimsy nylon down her legs and off her feet.

The stockings were next. Victor took the left leg, I the right. Cupping her firmly around the thigh, my fingers pressing into the smooth soft innerflesh, I unclipped the nylon from the stays of the garter belt. Slowly I slid it down her columnar leg, trailing the descending nylon with my hands, savoring the sweeping curves of her shapely leg. The garter belt was the last item to go.

Next we re-tied her, legs spread, feminine charms once more on display. Now she was

totally naked, completely open to our probing eyes, our hands, our cocks. I noticed her
chest was heaving, the gentle swells of her
breasts rising and falling in her growing
excitement.

Now Victor and I positioned ourselves on
either side of the straining form and, passing
the bottle of oil, poured the syrupy liquid
over our hands. I also let a stream fall onto
the tautly-stretched body, hitting her flat belly,
splashing her cunt and tits.

Then we started in on her. We began at the
wrists rubbing the oil all along her arms, over
her shoulders, and on into her open armpits.
She started to stir as our hands continued on
down her sleek sides and along her flanks to
her hips. We kept pace with one another,
working slowly around the front of her streamlined body to the smooth expanse of velvety
flesh below the breasts. Ashley's long lashes
fluttered down. She curled her lower lip, biting it gently, indenting the soft flesh with two
tiny teeth as a whimper escaped her. Our
hands moved up to capture the flattened
mounds of her tits.

We spent a lot of time there, oiling her
boobs thoroughly. Victor massaged, pulled and
stretched the pliant flesh of her left breast,
while I rubbed and played with her right one.
The tormented blond, her eyes clenched tight,
was rolling her head from side to side, mum-
bling incoherently, locked in her inner world
of passion. We tweaked her fat pink nipples,
pulling on the little stems, flicking them back

and forth, causing her to squirm as she tried to raise her chest, forcing her burning boobs deeper into our teasing hands. Now she was twisting her shoulders, urging us on, alternately pushing up with her right tit and her left. We ignored her demands, playing with her tits then stopping perversely, then attacking again, as we fondled her randomly, at our whim.

When we had satisfied ourselves that her tits had been well-oiled, we moved on, our hands exploring her torso, hips, and thighs. I trailed my fingers across her taut belly, which flinched at the teasing touch. I traced a line across the even plain onto the ridge of her right hip, and down her sleek haunches then around a firmly rounded thigh, watching the inner sinews twitch at my intimate touch. Till now I had avoided her sex, but that was my next stop. I cupped her twat and rubbed my palm against her crotch, soaking the tiny curls with oil, rubbing it into the soft folds of her pussy. She sighed, a long deep sigh, as my hand pressed on her cunt.

Now our blond captive was writhing and thrashing in her bonds. Clenching her teeth she whipped her head from side to side in demented fury; long silky strands beating on the tabletop. Her groans were deepening now, becoming more urgent, a plea for release from the unrelenting stimulation. Suddenly, she strained her hips upward, tensing against her restraints. Then she started bucking her hips, humping up and down in a driven fucking motion, all the while pleading with us, begging us to fuck her.

I renewed my attack on her pussy, while Victor grabbed both tits, viciously twisting the slick knobs. The girl hollered and yelled, cursing at the top of her voice, and climaxed in a huge shudder followed by repeated spasmodic throbs which shook her outstretched body. Then she was gasping for air, gulping in great heaves. A shiver ran through her body; her soft moans subsiding as she sunk into the warmth of afterglow.

She lay there with eyes closed, features calm, perfectly still except for her gradually subsiding breasts. But she would not be permitted to rest, not while our needs were left unattended to.

As she lay there trying to regain her breath, we slipped out of pants and briefs, taking up positions even with her head, our cocks rock-hard and demanding satisfaction.

"Come on, cunt, suck!" Victor commanded harshly.

Her eyes fluttered open, and she turned to him with a dazed uncomprehending look. Before she could respond, Victor was rubbing the head of his prick along her pretty face.

"Beg for it, bitch. Say 'fuck my face,'" he screamed at her.

"Oh yes, fuck my face, fuck my face," she breathed throatily.

Obediently, she opened her mouth and had it stuffed with hard throbbing cock. He let her work him over for maybe half a minute, then he pulled out, nodding at me. I grabbed a handful of silken hair, and yanked her face around towards me, wanting, desperately wanting to fuck her face. I found the girl had a quick and lively tongue, and I let her mouth fondle my straining prick almost to the boiling point.

Then Victor and I, our upstanding pricks glistening with her saliva, and swaying in the air, went about untying her wrists. I took one of the blond's hands and placed it on my cock; Victor did the same. She knew what to do. Soon she was entering into the spirit of the thing, gripping us tightly. I felt her talons dig into my hard prick as she clutched the shaft and squeezed. Then she was jerking us off, pumping her little fists up and down with frenzied urgency.

It didn't take much of that before I was close to shooting my wad. As I felt my boiling sperm rising, I pulled away from her tight grip, aiming my prick at her proud aristocratic face. Victor did the same, and together we spurted thick gobs of cum onto her forehead, splattering her eyes, nose, and mouth. Victor even managed to hit her ear. She moaned and let out a piercing shriek, and somewhat surprisingly, had a second shuddering orgasm right there as the cum rained down on her contorted face.

*   *   *

Victor and I slumped down on one of the wooden benches, and lit cigarettes. He had brought a bottle of wine with him, and we poured ourselves a couple of glasses. As we sat there, drinking wine and smoking, I wondered aloud if we should share some with our blond captive. Victor's response was to pour two more glasses, then go over and shove the bottle up Ashley's well-lubricated cunt. The exhausted blond jerked reflexively at the sudden intrusion, and made a little gurgling sound deep in her throat. Otherwise, she lay still, her legs straddling the hard bottle wedged between her thighs, as we talked about the next act in our little drama.

Victor, looking over at the sprawled form, suggested we have her fuck herself with the bottle. We told Ashley what we wanted, but the bedraggled female didn't stir. So we propped her up into a half-sitting position, and placed her hands on the bottle, shoving it in and urging her on. In a moment she was working the neck of the bottle in and out of her sopping wet cunt, her movements slow and languid. As we watched the gleaming neck emerging and disappearing Victor remarked that Ashley was one of those girls who would fuck anything. I proposed we try her out on the pillar.

This was a thick column about four feet around, covered with padding, and set at one end of the room. Inserted into the column, waist high, was a large protruding dildo, angled upward. When a girl is ordered to the column, she grabs two convenient handholds, wraps her legs around its ample girth and impales herself on the hard rubber shaft. Then grasping the column in a lover's embrace, she proceeds to fuck herself for the edification of the audience.

I untied Ashley while Victor greased the pole. As we led her over to the device, the frazzled blond seemed a little unsteady on her feet, still drained from her recent orgasms. We took her by the arms and helped her onto the shaft, Victor reaching down between her legs to open her sex up, while I gave her a shove on the ass. Now she was fixed in place, the dildo lodged up her cunt.

She turned to look at me, her eyes half-lidded, her hair soaked with sweat, disheveled, her face bathed in cum, and she smiled. I smacked her ass, and her eyes flew open in surprise as the dildo slid home into her well-soaked love nest.

Now she began riding her phantom lover clenching her thighs tightly, hollowing the sides of her buttocks, tensing her long haunches, seeking to bury the rod deeper into her hot churning depths. We watched the maddened rider gain her stride, a deep regular rhythmic motion, as she rode the fake cock, her hips plunging and grinding down against the padding. She was grunting with grim determination, intensely striving to bring herself off just one more time.

Suddenly, her head snapped back, her hair flailing wildly, as she let out one final piercing scream and thundered towards her third orgasm of the night.

*   *   *

Ashley was to come two more times that night. When the long session was over, she wasn't capable of moving, so we left her laying there naked and spent, asleep on the thick-pile carpet, with a contented smile on her cum-soaked face. We turned off the lights and straggled on up to bed.

CHAPTER EIGHT

At The Auction

The auction was the major event of the year at Ironwood. Invitations were sent all over the world to the selected list of Ironwood clients and their agents. The auction itself was always preceeded by a dinner which the new graduates were expected to attend as dinner companions of the guests.

In order to provide a more intimate atmosphere, and let the guests get to know their hostesses in a more personal way, clusters of small tables had been set in the dining room. Each table sat two diners, the privacy of the couple enhanced, although not insured, by a series of paneled partitions set up to form alcoves around each table.

In keeping with their new status, the young ladies were allowed to put aside their Ironwood uniform in favor of more elegant high-fashion gowns. These creations were imported from Paris or New York, but they were modi-

fied at Ironwood, cut so as to openly display
the breasts of the young debutantes. Thus
topless, and tastefully made up, their hair
elegantly arranged, these charming beauties
adorned our dinner tables.

For this occasion the younger girls were
assigned duties as waitresses. Like their older
sisters they performed their duties topless,
wearing just pantyhose and high heels. Their
sole article of decoration the high patent
leather collars edged with tiny sparkling
rhinestones.

Semi-nude, their bodies from waist down
encased in smoky-tinted nylon, they presented
an alluring picture. As they scurried about,
waiting on tables in their erotic costumes, they
drew a fair share of attention from the guests
as roving hands captured a swaying tit, caressed a nylon-clad haunch, or playfully swat-
ted a convenient behind, as the girl bent over
to serve a drink.

My dinner companion for the evening was
a vivacious, sensual girl named Joscelyn. Warm
and lively, Joscelyn had expressive eyes large
and amber-tinted, a wide generous mouth, a
ready smile, and soft auburn tresses, which
usually spilled down to just tease her shoulders. Tonight however, her hair was pinned
up, the deep, reddish brown coils shimmering
in the candlelight.

I studied her finely-drawn features in the
soft glow: her long, dark lashes over large
almond-shaped eyes, her comely smile with
the rich sensuous lips, and tiny white teeth,

the creamy smoothness of her bare neck and shoulders, and her sexy tits, two nicely-rounded globes, hanging temptingly, swaying slightly as she reached for her wine. In making her up for the evening, they had painted the wide disks of her aureoles with a dark red lipstick, so the tips gleamed wickedly in the shadows of the flickering candlelight.

Throughout the meal I managed to constrain myself from reaching over to feel up my charming dinner companion; not that she would have minded, still, I forced myself to wait, letting the tension slowly build. Finally, the dessert arrived and I could wait no longer. As our topless waitress was serving us dishes of rich smooth ice cream, I had an inspired idea.

Taking Joscelyn by the hand, I led her round the table to perch on my lap, her soft warmth pressing against my hardon. Then I scooped up a handful of the dripping cold treat and mashed it squarely between her baubles. She let out a startled shriek and squirmed excitedly at the tingling cold of the frigid icy gob when it came into contact with her chest. I rubbed the stuff all over her boobs, around and between them, watching the crinkled nipples unfold and expand right before my eyes. Then I bent down to lick the frozen treat off her heavenly mounds. Cold and slightly minty the taste was delightful, as I laved her chest thoroughly, lapping around her swelling curves, along the crease in the undertuck of her boobs, up and over the rounded crest, and into the narrow valley between the dangling globes. Joscelyn was leaning back, her eyes closed dreamily, whimpering softly, and arching her back, offering up her succulent fruits to my greedy mouth.

When I had licked her tits clean, I had another idea. I had her stand, and grabbing her by the waist, lifted her up to sit her on the table, her nyloned legs dangling loosely over the edge. Then I worked her dress back up her legs, rucking it up all the way to her waist, as I pulled the material out from under her, leaving her pantied behind sitting directly on the table.

Now I stepped up between her legs, reached down to grab her panties at each hip, and tugged the nylon down her legs and off over her high heels. Next I pushed her on the chest, forcing her back on her elbows. Placing my hands on the smooth insides of the thighs, I pushed her legs apart to lay open her cunt, her pareted furrow in its thicket of auburn curls. Next, I placed a dish of ice cream between her legs.

"Here's a little dessert for your cunt. Go on, shove it up your twat," I ordered handing her a large soupspoon.

She looked up at me uncertainly but with a crooked half-smile. Joscelyn was always ready for some new game. She took the spoon in her right hand, as with her left, she reached down to open up her netherlips. Then, holding the fleshy gates apart between her splayed fingers, she scooped up a gob of the slightly melted ice cream, and spooned it into her gaping cunt. She winced and let out an involuntary "oooh," shivering from shoulder to hips as the cold gooey mass was shoved up into her hot cuntal channel. She looked at me quizzically.

"Go on, all of it!" I ordered, responding to her unspoken question.

She scooped up a second spoonful and plastered it against her sex, tamping the icy dessert deep into her core. I watched her sitting there legs spread, feeding her cunt, spooning in the gooey mass, intent on what she was doing. Her head was bent forward. Her earlier exertions had caused a few wispy strands of hair to fall out of place and down along her slightly flushed face. The tiny brown hairs around the rim of her pussy were lathered with the melting yellow cream oozing from her twat.

Impatiently, I stood up and, clearing the dishes out of the way, clamped a hand on each naked shoulder, slowly forcing her over on her back. Then I knelt between her legs, running my hands under her, up the backs of her rounded thighs, grabbing her by the asscheeks, to pull her crotch towards me.

Slowly, lovingly, I began licking the sweet goo from around her pussy. The inner walls of her thighs were wet and sticky with the stuff. I covered every inch of that smooth flesh, lapping up the wet syrup in long broad strokes. After I had gotten all around her cavern, cleaning off the soft folds, the outer

lips, and the tiny hairs, I was ready to zero in
on her core.

I used both hands to pry her thighs apart
while I strained to touch the tip of my tongue
to the cold chill oozing from her twat. Lapping and sucking I used my tongue to get at
the ice cream, savoring the intriguing taste of
the sweet cold cream mixed with the tangy
nectar of her girl juices.

Naturally all this tongue action was having
its effect on my auburn beauty, who was
squirming, shimmying her ass, sliding from
side to side, and making whimpering sounds
like a kitten. Unable to control herself she
reached down and, grabbing me by the ears,
pulled my face deeper into her, jamming my
mouth against her crotch. She raised her legs,
bending her knees further and opening up
her thighs to the limits in an effort to force
still greater penetration. Her thighs began to
quiver, then suddenly spasomed, clamping
against the side of my head as she went rigid,
her hips straining upwards. She mewed, tight-
lipped, and squeezed my face with her thighs,
coming with a final convulsive shudder.

*   *   *

At the conclusion of the dinner a gong was
sounded and the young ladies were excused
to prepare themselves to take their places in
the ballroom. The first stage of the auction
was designed to give the guests the opportunity to sample our wares at first hand, to
closely inspect and compare the women whom
Ironwood would be offering for sale later

that evening. For this purpose the ballroom
had been cleared of all furniture, and a large
red curtain installed between the pillars set at
the far side.

As the guests began to file into the ballroom, the lights were dimmed, the drapes lit
by a series of floodlights. When the last guests
had entered, the curtain was drawn back to
reveal seven cute feminine bottoms lined up
in a row.

For this display a series of wooden stocks
had been set up side by side. These were
standing stocks, the type where the girl stepped
up to the board, bent over from the waist,
and placed her neck and wrists in semi-circular
cutouts. A hinged top board was then lowered and clamped shut, imprisoning her in
the stocks. To make their intimate parts more
accessible, each girl's legs were held apart by
a short spreader bar secured between ankle
cuffs.

The guests now approached the bent forms
to more closely inspect the display of feminine charms. They were encouraged to test
the reactions of the presented females, to apply various stimulants to the proferred behinds. The girls could not, of course, see their
tormentors, but to assure the element of surprise they had been blindfolded. For obvious
reasons, they had also been gagged.

Thus prepared, they were at the complete
disposal of any curious guest who might wish
to satisfy any bizarre whim. For their further
amusement, the guests were provided with an

assortment of helpful instruments. Two large tables had been set up to one side, and on these had been placed a wide variety of implements, some commonplace, some unusual, which the guests might choose to employ in amusing themselves with the displayed female anatomy.

The guests milled about, a few rummaging through the objects on the table. Gradually, individually and in small groups, they sauntered over to inspect the charming display. I joined a little group gathered around a certain Ferdnand D., a Frenchman I knew to be of impeccable manners. Monsieur D. had chosen a stiff feather with which to torment the firm, rounded buttocks of a restrained blond.

Deliberately, the fastidious Frenchman placed his left hand on top of the protruding mounds, resting it firmly, while he examined the proferred ass at close range, the wicked feather held at the ready in his right hand. The firm twin hemispheres were deeply divided: the bottom crease, separating her ass from her thighs, a pronounced double curve. Further below, in the hidden valley of her crotch, one could discern a few stray pussyhairs, a light fuzz of blond, that seemed vaguely familiar.

With his left hand Monsieur D. gently tapped the jutting swells just over their centers. The bent girl remained motionless.

Then he introduced her to the feather by placing it up between the rounded columns of her legs and setting the tip against the satiny innerflesh of her left thigh. At the feathery touch, I saw a ripple run through the muscles of the thigh. Very slowly her tormentor let the teasing tip trail down the smooth wall. I watched a series of tiny quivers spasm through her inner thighs as he tickled her there, high up between her legs.

Now the teasing tip was moving onto her sex, kissing the slight bulge of her hanging pouch, stretched open by her widened stance. The feathery tip raced back and forth in the groove, barely brushing the springy coils of hair, whispering over the secret passages of her lightly-furred vulva.

His victim was squirming excitedly now, her hips making little thrusting movements, as she was half-tickled, half-aroused by the sweet torture of the relentless quill. Then the meticulous Frenchman found the center seam and drew the tip along that short ridge from her ass to her cunt hole.

The sudden goose elicited a startled jerk by his surprised little playmate. I looked around to the front of the board. Her little fists were clenched and lines of intense concentration crossed her forehead. The long blond hair, imprisoned by the bands holding blindfold and gag, fell in some disarray.

By now the Frenchman had neared his target, the dusky pink slot, stretched open by the wide-spread legs. I squatted down to get a better look as he rimmed the taut lips along the edge of yawning cunthole.

Her hips were shaking uncontrollably now, and Monsieur D. politely asked for my assistance. I put my arm around her hips to steady her trembling loins as the tip slowly worked its way into her dark cavern. Now he stabbed it into her hole, twirling the feather between thumb and forefinger while keeping it deep in her hot box.

By this point, I could barely hold her, her hips were shaking wildly as the captive girl humped up and down on the slender reed tickling her inner recesses. The muffled gurgling sound we heard coming from the other end was rising in intensity and it was obvious that our little playmate was nearing a powerful orgasm.

At this crucial moment the devilish Frenchman chose to remove the probing feather from her love core. It came out wet with her juices, and he held it under his nose for a long whiff, offering it to me next. The quill reeked of the pungent smell of feminine arousal.

Once again he asked my assistance by requesting that I place a hand on each asscheek and open her up. Prying the soft rubbers apart revealed the amber-tinted center crease, and the puckered dimple of her asshole, all laid open and vulnerable to the ubiquitous feather.

Teasingly, he ran the feathery intruder up and down the narrow strip of sensitive flesh, sending her flinching, jerking her hips forward in violent reaction at the maddening tickle. Her butt muscles tightened spasmodically, straining to clamp on the tantalizing shaft, but my hands held her cheeks apart, thumbs inserted deep, pressing into the soft mounds. The tormenting feather must have driven her to a frenzy as the Frenchman zeroed in on the little rubbery ring of muscle, delicately inserting the tip and screwing it in. The tormented blond was thrashing uncontrollably now, testing the limits of her restraints, shaking her ass wildly against my firm grip.

The cries coming from behind the gag turned into muffled shrieks. Then unexpectedly she stopped moving, a low moan coming from behind the gag. Suddenly the rigid muscles in the backs of her thighs slackened and she sagged slightly. The strong odor of her arousal permeated the air in the aftermath of her orgasm. I noticed the insides of her thighs were wet, covered with a sheen of perspiration mingled with her copious sexual spendings.

The amused Frenchman grinned wickedly at me and winked as he turned the lethal feather around, and viciously drove the pointy end right up her ass. We left her like that, spent, sagging motionless, the long white feather between her rearcheek, sticking straight out obscenely. We moved on to join the action further down the line.

*   *   *

The next female who was providing amusement for the guests was a rather obvious brunette, obvious since her low slung pussy with its thicket of tiny curls was just visible from behind. She was being attended to by two ladies, one of whom, an older rather severe blond, was the owner of a very exclusive house of pleasure tucked away in New York's east side.

They each held a vibrator to be used on the vulnerable behind. The girl shifted slightly patiently awaiting their ministrations.

The brunette's mounds were two gentle swells, slightly pendulous, their heart-shape made more obvious by her stance. Her skin was dusky and smooth. This cuddly handful was receiving careful attention from the two fashionably dressed ladies, who retained their long gloves as they caressed the asscheeks, squeezing and poking the spongy flesh, and lewdly commenting on their resiliency.

The blond began the serious work of stimulation by running the penis shaped vibrator down the backs of the thighs of the dusky beauty. I watched her tight muscles ripple and shimmy as the tiny vibrations coursed through them. She now ran the shaft along the undercrease and up onto the bottom of her swells, digging it into the soft yielding flesh which trembled and shook like jello under the deep massage.

Now the blond tormentor ran the thick shaft down the shadowy center crease and under her arch, clamping the buzzing toy tightly against the soft pussyfolds. This stimulated a fury of hip action on the part of the captive brunette as she squatted a little, trying in vain to trap the shaft between her hungry thighs. Then the blond switched tactics and advanced directly on the stretched-open cunt hole. The vibrator moved along the netherlips, teasing the fleshy little gates, before it disappeared into the gaping hole. The blond shoved it home and turned the humming shaft, screwing it into her victim.

In the meantime, her friend had activated her little toy. This was a rectal vibrator, pencil thin and about six inches long. While the blond tightened her grip on the plastic shaft buried deep in the girl's cunt, she stepped to one side, giving her companion easier access to the girl's bottom.

I watched a black-gloved hand reach over, spanning the rearcheeks just at the top, and forcing open the rubbery mounds. Then the slender rod was placed against the sensitive inner flesh just above the tiny grommet, sending vibrations coursing through the soft wobbling mounds and driving the brunette into a demented frenzy. Her pinioned legs thrashed about, her ass shaking and squirming at the double stimulation. With clinical detachment the rectal vibrator was slowly inserted, pushing against the tight-ringed muscle until it yielded, accepting the long thin rod.

The ladies took a minute to stand back and admire their handiwork, leaving the vibrators in place. With both her cunt and her ass plugged with several inches of hard vibrating plastic, the shaking female was being driven half-mad by the flood of sensations surging up from her nether regions.

Her body was jerking rhythmically now, her ass bouncing backward and forward. We heard a muffled scream, although we couldn't be sure it was from her, since there were a good many muted sounds of passion in the room at the moment.

I watched entranced as convulsive shudders racked her body; then she was still. Only the muted buzzing sound remained, the shafts still firmly embedded in place, as she slumped in her bonds. I believe the intentions of the ladies were to leave the two active vibrators in place to see how long it would take to arouse the girl a second time. I moved on.

*   *   *

The next proferred ass was small, white, and tight-cheeked. The narrow centercrease neatly divided the two shiny hemispheres. From the sprinkling of black pussyhair just visible between her legs, I speculated as to who the straining girl might be.

The lovely swells of her out-thrust young bottom so invitingly displayed, obviously suggested that hers was an ass made for spanking. And that thought seems to have occurred to the two guests who stood there studying it now. I knew them as the M. brothers, Arabs from one of the small Persian Gulf states. They were valued clients of ours, with rather bizarre tastes. One was never quite sure what would arouse their attention where women were concerned.

At the moment the two shieks were armed with flyswatters. Each had positioned himself just to the side of a jutting cheek, and they were whipping the rounded contours with small flicks of the wrist. The spanking was not hard, just a constant little tattoo, a relentless flutter of swats right on the soft, malleable, and very vulnerable behind.

I watched the female shift uncomfortably from one foot to the other and back again, under the constant pitter-patter of light taps. Her cheeks were taking on a rosy glow, as the brothers kept up their single-minded efforts. They concentrated on the centers of the rounded domes, then moved to the top, the bottom and even underneath to smack the backs of her trim thighs, leaving the flesh reddened and warm.

Finally, having tired of their efforts, they dropped their weapons to devote themselves to fondling the newly-punished female bottom. Then, suddenly inspired, one of them picked up a decorative Union Jack, which was lying on the table, and inserted the tiny flagpole up her ass.

They stepped back to better appreciate the tableau, laughing and hugging each other as they chattered in Arabic. I left them joking and pointing at the reddened ass, with the little flag hanging out from between her tight, clenching cheeks.

I strolled on, trooping the line, stopping here and there to observe some bizarre scene as an imaginative guest made some ingeneous use of the handy female anatomy. I reflected that we probably had some of the most inventive sexual enthusiasts in the world gathered in this one room.

* * *

The girls spent two hours in their restraints, having their asses, cunts, and hanging tits played with unmercifully; their feminine charms caressed, tortured, teased, and tormented. When finally released from their restraints, they were led off stiff, spent, and sore. They would be allowed an hour to rest, their recovery aided by a generous allotment of brandy to revive them, so they would be ready for the main event.

In the interim, the guests were served drinks, while two rows of chairs were set up in a semicircle facing the curtain. Once again the house lights dimmed, and you could sense the excitement as the crowd waited for the final act to begin.

With their usual theatrical flair, Cora had arranged a dramatic entrance. The curtain was pulled back to reveal a bare, floodlit stage. Then Cora made her appearance, characteristically dressed all in black. In her left hand she clenched a riding crop, in her right a set of reins, and in front of her, attached to those reins, were two little females, crawling forward on hands and knees. I recognized these pubescent blonds as the little imps who had been assigned erotic duties as they crouched under the table during the class on deportment. Now they were naked, their little hanging breasts swaying as they scrambled forward, straining against the gleaming harnesses and tight reins. Cora walked her pets around the stage like a pair of bitches out for a stroll with their mistress. She slapped the riding crop against her thigh, but she didn't use it on the shifting behinds.

After making several circuits, she unleashed her little escorts who scurried about to take their positions at each side of the stage.

They sat back on their legs, feet tucked under their soft behinds, their arms rigid at their sides supporting them as they threw back their shoulders, and stared out over the audience. The pose gave a delightful view of their golden manes, slim shoulders, small tits and little blond bushes just visible below. They seemed a parody of stone lions guarding the entrance to some library.

Now the stage was set for the graduation procession. This was led by Monique who, like Cora, had dressed all in black, with high stiletto shoes, and a riding crop in her left hand. Wrapped around her right gloved hand was a silver chain. The other end of that chain had been attached to the collar of the first of a string of young women. The graduates had been serially linked one to another, by the tethering chain attached in turn to a leather collar snapped around each pretty neck.

In true slave style their arms were secured behind their backs by wrist straps linked together. Similar straps encircled their ankles. Except for the leather straps and high heels, they were totally naked.

They shuffled onto the stage, their heads lowered. At a command from Monique they turned as one to face the audience, then they went down on their knees, eyes downcast, in the familiar pose of submission, to await their turns on the auction block.

The auction block was actually a raised circular platform placed at the center of the stage. Once the tableau had been established it was up to me, in my roles as master of ceremonies and auctioneer, to begin the proceedings.

My job was to put each girl through her paces, a more or less standard routine, designed to show off her best features. I took my position near the stage. The floodlights dimmed leaving a single spotlight bathing the circle. The first girl to take center stage was the lovely Jacqueline.

Cora stepped up to her and leaned down to murmur a few words in the girl's ear as she unsnapped the collar from the tethering chain. Jackie kept her eyes straight ahead, her face expressionless. With splendid dignity the lithe blond slowly stepped up into the spotlight.

I started with a brief introduction, as Jackie stood motionless, the light shining on her golden hair, bathing her slender shoulders and the tops of her high-set breasts, casting shadows down her long willowy body. When I finished the introduction, I began the drill.

First I had her lean forward from the waist so that her breasts hung down underneath, elongating into little tit-bags. I had her wriggle her shoulders, jiggling the small dangling weights. Maintaining the pose I had her cup her breasts, caressing them, offering them up to the silent audience. I watched her long fingers, her nails painted a dark brownish-red, capture the little globes and squeeze the soft flesh. Then she was made to tweak the nipples, pulling and stretching them, causing them to stiffen under the stimulation, all the while keeping her eyes on the hungry audience.

Next I had her straighten up, hands on hips, spread her legs and begin to lean backwards. Bending her knees and thrusting out her pussy, with its small blond bush, straight at her audience, she slowly lowered herself backwards. With athletic ease, she dropped her hands to the floor behind her to support herself, her supple body bowed in an erotic display. The pose gave her audience a view of her little love purse tucked deep between her straining thighs, its pastel pink cleve slightly parted by her outstretched thighs. Her leg muscles quivered with tension as she struggled to hold the pose, throwing back her head, letting her soft blond strands fall behind to sweep the floor.

Taking pity on her in the demanding position, I let her get down on her knees and bend backwards, supporting herself on one hand while she reached around with the other to open her sex for her most appreciative audience. This obscene pose gave them an enticing view of her cunt, the stretched nether-lips, swollen and flushed, the glistening pink of the inner walls, the dark hole at the center, and the soft cloud of pale blond curls marking her light-furred vulva.

Her next set of poses were designed to allow the audience to appreciate the rear view. Standing tall, her hands loosely at her sides, she turned her back to the audience. Now the light fell on those slim shoulders, the smooth even slope of her back sweeping out into the gentle swells of her cute bottom, over the mounds and down the long sweeping contours of her slender legs. Trim and lissome, the sight of this alluring beauty brought back a flood of sweet memories.

I ordered her to touch her toes, and she bent low, her ass thrust out at the audience. Next she was ordered to show her asshole. Without hesitation, her slender arms reached behind her, her hands clasping her cheeks firmly. I watched her long fingers move across the mounds, the pointed red fingernails digging into the flesh at the center, as she pulled the crease open, revealing her tiny pink rose to the avid eyes of her audience.

I let her stand like that for several minutes, bent over, her ass thrust out for all to see. The audience was treated to this erotic scene of unabashed nakedness; the girl's most intimate secret revealed for all to see.

For the last act of each presentation, the girl was to give a little performance. Jacqueline would be made to play with herself. A small settee was brought out and placed with one end towards the audience. The compliant blond languidly draped herself over the cushions, laying on her back, a pillow under her ass, and letting her legs dangle over the end facing the silent audience.

She lay her head back and closed her eyes as she brought her hands up the long willowy lines from hips to the high-set globes. She caressed herself there for a few minutes, molding the soft flesh, fondling her tits, slowly creating a sense of rising sexual tension in the quiet room. We watched her hands give up her tits and inch slowly down the slight indentation of her taut belly, her fingers just nosing into the small bush of her jutting love-mound.

Now, with liquid, sensuous movements, she spread her long legs apart, shifting her hips on the black velvet. We saw the searching fingers, their red nails gleaming wickedly, slide over the mound and into the soft folds between her thighs. Then she was rubbing herself there, her palm placed firmly against her pudendum. She moved her hand in small circular massage. I watched as lines of urgency began to crease her pretty face. Her eyes clenched tight, as she entered deeper into her own secret pleasure world, while the audience watched in mesmerized silence.

Then the fingers were moving again, restless and probing, with a renewed sense of urgency. She slipped two fingers down along her pussyslit rubbing the lips a little. Then holding herself open with one hand, she moistened two fingers in her mouth and placed the fingertips near her clitoris. We watched entranced as the teasing fingertips lightly rubbed the pearl of her clit peering out from beneath its hood of soft innerflesh. Her lips were parted; her deep labored breathing clearly audible in the hushed room.

Her hand curled up under her open sex and she inserted the long center finger into her slot. It was joined by two more; three fingers disappearing up her snatch. We watched her stiffened fingers drive in and out, the digits glistening now with her copious spendings. Soon she was moving sensuously, snaking her hips, and moving her head slowly from side to side, her face contorted as in pain.

Her movements became more vigorous, her plunging hand more energetic as she strained to lift her hips high up off the pillow, her head wildly tossing from side to side, beating the black velvet with her silky strands. Her face was flushed with sexual excitement, her jaw clenched tight, and I could see sweat breaking out on her forehead, as she rode her pistoning hand to the brink.

Now she was thrashing about insanely, driven to a sexual frenzy by the penetrating fingers of her right hand. Caught in the throes of passion, she surrendered to the radiating waves of pleasure coming from her hot cunt. Then an urgent intense look came over her pretty features as her face contorted in erotic pleasure. Her hips rose to their topmost height, straining while her torso arched back. A convulsive spasm slammed through her slim frame, and she moaned, a long lingering plaintive cry. Then the girl sank back onto the soft velvet, laying perfectly still, her face soft and content in the dreamy aftermath of her shuddering climax.

There was a moment of silence, then the stunned audience burst into hearty applause. After that the bidding started and, not surprisingly, it started quite high. Later Cora and I, counting the receipts, agreed that it had been one of our most successful auctions ever.

CHAPTER NINE

Cora Redux

It was late in the morning. We were working together in the office at Ironwood. I sat behind the desk; Cora by my side, crisp and efficient in a plain white blouse, neatly tailored skirt, and dark stockings.

We had been going over the financial statements, and Cora was pointing out some item on the spreadsheet. She leaned down as we examined the papers more closely, bringing her face nearer to mine. I caught the scent of the light fragrance she wore. I glanced up at her to find her arresting blue eyes waiting for mine. She stopped abruptly in mid-sentence while our eyes locked on each other's, her face just inches from mine.

"What is it, Cora," I urged.

"I ... uh ... wanted to say something, James," she began haltingly, suddenly flustered. Her eyelashes fluttered and she averted her eyes to avoid my gaze.

"It's ... it's just that you'll soon be gone again, and we hardly saw each other since you returned. And ... that is ... well ... I need you, James. Can't we spend some time together?" The last tumbled out in a rushed whisper.

"I'm not sure I understand what it is you want, Cora," I pretended. "I wonder if you know yourself. Tell me, explain it to me, what is it you really want, Cora. What is it you need?" I teased.

A tinge of color rose to the cheeks of the embarrassed female. Uncharacteristically, she seemed uncertain and confused, looking at me beseechingly. But I wasn't going to make it any easier for her. I simply waited for her to go on. She understood the game and what was required of her, the need to say it, to willingly debase herself. Her tongue flickered out, nervously flitting over her lips. She tried again.

"I need you, James. I need you ... to take me, to fuck me. You can do whatever you want with me, only let me obey you, please, James, please," she hissed.

I remained motionless, scanning her face, waiting for more, while the humiliated mistress of Ironwood blushed furiously.

"That's not the Ironwood way to request a favor, you know that. Now do it properly," I commanded.

Without hesitation, the elegant blond lowered herself to her knees, the nylon rasping on the carpeted floor. Her gaze was level with my crotch now, and she kept her eyes there as she began yet once more to plead with me.

"Please, Master James, use me, use me in any way that will give you pleasure. Force me to obey your will," she mumbled in a low whisper, her blond head lowered submissively, her eyes fixed on my crotch the whole while. Gone was the image of the crisp, self-confident businesswoman. This was the different Cora, on her knees before me, more real, more elemental. I knew she found it all intensely humiliating, yet I also knew it was exciting her beyond belief, fulfilling her deep desire to be subjugated. I have found that some women, particularly those who love to control others, have such an underlying need to be dominated. Like Cora, most are only vaguely aware of that need. But I had taken Cora once before, subjecting her will to mine, and in so doing, had forced her to confront her strange desire, that burning need, that only a dominant male could satisfy. Now she understood herself, knew these vague stirrings for what they were. That was why she was on her knees. That was why she pleaded with me not to deny her satisfaction.

I looked down at the blond who knelt motionless, docilely waiting to do my bidding.

"You are to wait in my room for my return this afternoon. I want you as you are now, on your knees, but naked, except for one item of adornment. You are to fetch a pair of nipple clamps to wear for me. When I come in I want to see you naked, on your knees, with

the clamps hanging from your tits. Now go.
I've got work to do," I dismissed her curtly,
turning back to my papers.

Out of the corner of my eye, I watched the
tall blond gather herself to her full height,
slowly turn, and, dream-like, silently glide from
the room to carry out my orders.

*   *   *

I lingered over a superb lunch that day, lit
a cigar, and poured myself another cup of
coffee. I knew that Cora, uncertain as to when
I might return, would be waiting for me in
my room. I decided to let her wait, letting the
anticipation build for both of us.

In time I leisurely sauntered back to my
room opening the door to behold a splendid
view: the naked blond figure kneeling erect
in the middle of the room, the sunlight of early
afternoon streaming over her exquisite form.
She must have been sitting on her haunches
waiting, but she stiffened and straightened
up at the sound of the opening door, holding
herself erect and tense.

I walked in and, without a word, began
shedding my clothes. Slowly I stripped, letting her watch me, but ignoring her all the
while. When I was naked I walked over to the
closet and selected a short silk robe. Then I
approached the kneeling form, pulling a chair
around to place it a few feet directly in front
of her. I sat down and lit a cigarette, studying the naked body and contemplating a delightful afternoon.

I stared at her pendulous boobs, round,

full, sagging slightly, and crowned by two thick pink disks. She had used the screw clamps for the self-punishment that I had imposed on her. These were tiny screw-clamps which were tightened down on the nipples, pinching the flesh, distending the engorged nubs. The little weights hanging on her chest must have caused her some discomfort, but I knew they would be nothing like the pain of the tiny alligator clips she sometimes liked to experiment with on her charges. I was not surprised that she had selected the milder screw-clamps for herself.

She watched as I reached down to place my fingertips along the soft contour at the top of her left breast. She was already excited, breathing through parted lips, her breasts rising in mounting swells. I traced a line from the upper curve down to the biting clamp. Lifting the tiny weight with my fingertips, I bounced it gently, watching the fleshy nipple being stretched, elongated. Cora whimpered, biting her lower lip to keep from crying out. Then I grabbed the clamp and pulled, stretching out the pliant flesh until she winced in pain, gasping with a sharp hiss. I wanted to hurt her. Viciously, I turned my wrist, twisting the tortured nipple, till unable to bear the pain in silence, she cried out.

"What's the matter, bitch? Does it hurt?" I demanded menacingly. "Tell me about it," I said, slowly twisting the other clamp on her right tit.

"Oh, yes . . . yes . . . it hurts so much when

you twist my tits like that," she hissed, the words tumbling out as her face contorted in pain.

"Well, perhaps if you ask nicely, I might allow you to remove them, at least for now."

"Yes, Master James, oh please yes . . . may I take off these beastly clamps, please?" she pleaded, her low whisper taking on an urgent tone.

"Alright, you may take them off, and hand them to me."

With great care she removed the tormenting screws. The tortured nipples darkened, swelling and stiffening as the blood surged back into the pinched tips. She raised her hands to soothe her irritated nipples, swollen with pain, yet stiff with obvious sexual excitement. Already it was getting to her, and we had only just begun.

"Come over here, I want to beat your ass," I snarled.

She arose a little unsteadily, and approached me with downcast eyes, totally acquiescent as she draped her long body over my lap, her warm hip pressing against my stirring cock. I let my hand rest on the lovely swells of her upturned bottom, trailing my fingers over the satiny smooth rearcheeks, digging my fingers into the spongy flesh, clamping one of the rounded domes, gripping her firmly and crushing the meaty mound. Cora cried out, jerked upwards, and squirmed against my upstanding prick.

Without further ado, I hauled back and

struck, smacking her hard, my palm stinging, as I delivered a punishing blow to her proferred behind. She jerked a little at each swat, as her soft swells wobbled and subsided like a bowl of jello. I watched her clamp her cowering cheeks, forming supple hollows in her long lean haunches as she tightened her butt muscles, preparing herself to receive the next slap.

I attacked her vulnerable ass with grim determination now, spanking her again and again, flattening the resilient cushions, getting a grunt at each blow from the upsidedown head. Now I switched tactics, using a series of short, rapid-fire smacks, as she flopped about on my lap, flailing her legs and kicking wildly. I placed a firm hand on the small of her back to steady her as I continued, the slaps echoing in the still room, as I struck the quivering, cringing, reddened flesh; slapping sounds mingling with her piteous cries.

I spanked her heaving reddened asscheeks until my arm got tired and my hand hurt. Then I decided to finish the job in a way that would be less painful—for me. Abruptly, I jumped up, dumping the moaning woman on the carpet.

She started to pick herself up, but I placed my foot squarely on her warm ass and pressed down, pinning her to the floor.

"Stay," I commanded, picking up a set of binding straps which I had collected earlier in the punishment chamber.

Now I proceeded to tie her up. Placing her arms against her sides, I circled her long torso, binding her arms to her sleek sides. The first strap went around her upper arms and just over the tops of her breasts. The second one ran around her waist, pinioning her arms just below the elbows, securing them tightly against her sides. I placed the third strap directly over her ample breasts, and when I cinched it tight in back, it squeezed those lovely globes, indenting the soft flesh, distorting the pretty shapes. As I tightened the strap I watched her face. Lines of discomfort etched her brow and her upper teeth indented her lower lip as she clenched her jaw against the pain. She took it all without a word of protest.

The last thing I did was apply a ball gag, forcing it between her teeth, cinching it tightly in place through a buckle behind her head.

Now she was securely bound, the thin wicked strips cutting into the soft white flesh, her arms bound rigidly to her sides, immobilizing her upper body. The gag held her mouth open, her jaw slightly distended; her wide eyes a mixture of fear and growing passion.

I told her to get up. It wasn't easy but she managed to struggle to her feet unassisted. I grabbed her by the shoulders, and shoved her roughly towards one of the small bedroom chairs. When she was up against the back of it, I forced her to bend forward from the waist, over the back of the chair till her head touched the seat cushion. Her upthrust bottom presented a most tempting target.

Now I selected one of my favorite weapons, a thin yardstick, kept in my bedroom for just this purpose. I knew the whippy wood would impart a vicious sting to a feminine behind, having tried it out once or twice. Now I was ready for a full scale test of its effectiveness.

Stepping up to one side of Cora's lush orbs, I reached back and swung. The lath bit in the soft flesh with a crack like a rifle shot. The force of the blow caused her to bounce up on her toes, as a strangled cry emerged from the gagged mouth.

It must have stung painfully for a thin red welt appeared crossing both cheeks right at the center. Now I let her have it again, and again, timing my blows, waiting for her cringing cheeks to slacken, then striking. There was a constant muffled scream coming from the punished female as she squirmed her hips, in a futile effort to keep the blows from falling squarely on her blazing ass.

I paddled her two more times, the last blow a particularly vicious cut. Now she wore five distinct angry red stripes across her bottom. I peered at her face, and found tears running down her cheeks.

Standing behind her I placed a hand between her legs to cup her sex. She was hot and wet. Stiffening two fingers, I thrust into her, plunging in and out, making tiny squishing sounds in her well-lubricated cunt. Cora moaned softly. She was hurting, but she was obviously highly excited as I found out when I extracted my fingers to find them slick with evidence of her arousal. I wiped my hand across her face leaving a smear of feminine spendings, then grabbing a handful of silken hair to wipe my fingers.

Twisting my fingers in her hair, I used my hold to snap back her head. Then I placed my lips next to her ear.

"You're such a hot bitch, aren't you?" I murmured. "I think it's time we put out the fire."

So saying, I pushed her towards the bathroom. With a little effort I was able to get her into the tub. She lay there on her back, helplessly looking up at me, a vacant look in her passion-glazed eyes.

Looking down at her, I slowly slipped the robe from my shoulders.

Without a word, I stepped up to the edge of the tub, cock in hand, pointed it at her and let go. A steady stream of hot piss rained down on her helpless body. I aimed at her twat, her tits; finally, letting her have it in the face. She closed her eyes and tossed her head, as the golden shower pounded down on her, splashing her face, drenching her hair, a downpour that only gradually subsided to a trickle. I shook off the last few drops.

Cora lay motionless in the tub, eyes closed, piss dripping from her hair, running down her face, her eyes, her lips, down her long naked torso in rivulets, soaking her leather bonds.

I laughed, and leaned over to loosen her straps. Then I left her alone, telling her she had twenty minutes to clean herself up.

I fixed myself a drink while I waited for

her. In the background I could hear the shower running. She stepped out of the bathroom, warm and pink from her shower. She had that freshly-scrubbed look, her hair still a little damp. The marks from the leather bindings were fading from her arms, but her ass remained a vibrant pink. It would be sore for many days. She stepped into the bedroom and looked at me quizzically.

"You can get dressed now, but no pants."

She paused, taking that in for a moment.

"Panties and stockings?"

"No. Just your sweater and your heels, that's all."

I watched her dress, pulling the black turtleneck over her head, shaking her short hair into place with a casual gesture, running a brush through the short damp hair. She sat on the edge of a chair to slip a pair of patent leather heels on her bare feet.

She stood up and turned towards me, her hands at her sides. The black sweater, clinging to the curves of her upper body and slim arms, made a dramatic contrast with the succulent white flesh below. Naked from the waist down like that, her thick blond bush proudly displayed, her slender white haunches and long legs left uncovered, I found her terribly erotic.

I reached under my chair for the little toy I had laid there as a final surprise for her. It was a small thin butt plug, a hard rubber dildo, about the shape and thickness of a stubby pencil, with a flaring base.

I held it up to her face, staring into her wide blue eyes as I explained things to her.

"I've got something for you, bitch. You know what it is, and you know where it goes. Now I'm going to let you grease it up, so it's nice and smooth, then I'm going to shove it up your behind for you."

I saw a little shiver go through her at my words. She took the slender rod in her two hands, looking down on it like it was some foreign object she had never seen before. When she looked up at me, her eyes were once more glazed over in passion, her lips parted.

I watched her get the jar of vaseline and generously grease the shaft. Then she came to me and offered it up, almost reverently, as if we were engaged in some bizarre rite.

"Tell me where you want it," I whispered.

She lowered her eyes. I watched her lips as she formed the words. In a low, throaty voice she said, "Please, Master James, please shove it up my ass."

Grabbing her by the shoulders I had her stand facing the bed. I put a hand against her back and roughly pushed, shoving her forward, forcing her to throw out her hands to support herself, half bent over the mattress.

Clasping an ankle I forced her legs apart a little further. I couldn't resist those long shapely legs, and I passed a hand up and down one of the columnar lengths, feeling the smooth silky skin along the gentle curves from ankle to pussy.

"Spread your cheeks."

I wanted her to cooperate, to be actively involved in this, to help in her final humiliation. She let her upper body fall forward, her forehead resting on the mattress, as she reached back, grabbing her ass, pulling open the cheeks, and holding them apart for me. I placed my left hand on the small of her back to steady her, and with my right hand touched the greasy rod to her crinkled dimple, teasing it, watching it pucker in defensive reaction.

Then I slowly inserted the plug, inching it forward, while she made little urging sounds deep in her throat. The small ring of rubbery muscle contracted spasmodically, stretched by the hard shaft. I didn't force it. I waited for her to relax before I made her accept a little more, then a little more, as finally the whole rod was deep in her ass, the flat base sticking out lewdly between her well-punished cheeks.

There was one final detail to attend to. Leaving her there bent over, her ass sticking up in the air, I picked up a tangle of thin straps attached to a belt, which was used to hold the butt plug in place.

The leather straps were arranged so that when the belt was placed around the waist, one ran down behind bisecting the rearcheeks. At the underarch it split into a Y and two thin straps ran up each side of the girl's vulva, their ends attached to the belt in front. I placed the belt around Cora's waist just above the hips, telling her to take a deep breath and hold it, as I cinched the belt in place, constricting her soft flesh.

Next I reached down to grab the hanging center strap, pulling it through her underarch, and on up behind. I ran it through the clasp at the back of the belt, then I yanked on the strap giving it a couple of good tugs, to bury the leather deep into her crease. She emitted a single grunt, short and deep in her throat. Finally, I cinched it up, buckling it in back. The belt was securely in place now, snugly indenting the soft white flesh, assuring that the sturdy plug would remain firmly lodged up her behind.

I stepped back for a moment, running a finger along the straps to make sure they were tight against the flesh. In front the black strips nicely edged the smaller Vee of her blond vulva; in the back it was buried between the soft mounds. I had her take a seat, which she did very gingerly, her ass on the edge of the chair. I slapped her on the thigh and told her to spread her legs.

"Now listen to me, bitch. I put that little toy up your ass, and I'll be the one to take it out, when I'm good and ready. In the meantime, you'll wear it proudly. If nature calls, and you want it out, you'll come to me and ask my permission. Now get out of here, go back to work or whatever, I've got things to do."

She stayed there frozen to the spot, shocked and staring at me in wide-eyed wonder.

"But, James", she stammered, ". . . I can't go out like this. I mean I have work to do in the office, and we have dinner guests tonight, and then there are the girls to see to at pun-

ishment call. I can't let them see me like this,"
she pleaded.

I smiled.

"That's just the way I want you, bare-assed,
without those damn pants of yours. You might
be able to pull it off, if you stay seated behind
the desk, maybe no one will know. If you
have to get up, well, that might require some
explaining. Dinner's the same way. Stay seated,
maybe our guests won't notice. As to the girls,
sure they'll see it all, and they'll know what
you're wearing, but they'll understand. You
will tell them that your ass belongs to me, that
I shoved the little toy up there. Tell them it
pleases your master to have you so displayed,
your ass plugged tight. It will be a constant
reminder for you of who you are, and who
you belong to. They'll understand, because
they know the spirit of Ironwood. Now get
out and do what you were told!"

I waited. Staring at the woman who sat
there facing me, half-naked, her head bowed
in quiet acquiescence. We seemed to wait like
that for a long time.

At last she moved, slowly rising to her feet,
turning, and making her way to the door, her
long statuesque figure deliciously half-nude.
Her hand on the door, she turned to look
back at me, her adoring gaze softened by
abject loving surrender. I ignored her. Then
she opened the door and was gone. I heard
the measured click of her high heels receding
down the long hallway.

Order These Selected Blue Moon Titles

Souvenirs From a Boarding School $7.95	Shades of Singapore $7.95
The Captive $7.95	Images of Ironwood $7.95
Ironwood Revisited $7.95	What Love $7.95
Sundancer $7.95	Sabine $7.95
Julia $7.95	An English Education $7.95
The Captive II $7.95	The Encounter $7.95
Shadow Lane $7.95	Tutor's Bride $7.95
Belle Sauvage $7.95	A Brief Education $7.95
Shadow Lane III $7.95	Love Lessons $7.95
My Secret Life $9.95	Shogun's Agent $7.95
Our Scene $7.95	The Sign of the Scorpion $7.95
Chrysanthemum, Rose & the Samurai $7.95	Women of Gion $7.95
Captive V $7.95	Mariska I $7.95
Bombay Bound $7.95	Secret Talents $7.95
Sadopaideia $7.95	Beatrice $7.95
The New Story of O $7.95	S&M: The Last Taboo $8.95
Shadow Lane IV $7.95	"Frank" & I $7.95
Beauty in the Birch $7.95	Lament $7.95
Laura $7.95	The Boudoir $7.95
The Reckoning $7.95	The Bitch Witch $7.95
Ironwood Continued $7.95	Story of O $5.95
In a Mist $7.95	Romance of Lust $9.95
The Prussian Girls $7.95	Ironwood $7.95
Blue Velvet $7.95	Virtue's Rewards $5.95
Shadow Lane V $7.95	The Correct Sadist $7.95
Deep South $7.95	The New Olympia Reader $15.95

Visit our website at www.bluemoonbooks.com

ORDER FORM
Attach a separate sheet for additional titles.

Title	Quantity	Price
_____	____	____
_____	____	____
_____	____	____
_____	____	____

Shipping and Handling (see charges below) _____

Sales tax (in CA and NY) _____

Total _____

Name _____

Address _____

City _____ State _____ Zip _____

Daytime telephone number _____

❏ Check   ❏ Money Order   (US dollars only. No COD orders accepted.)

Credit Card # _____ Exp. Date _____

❏ MC   ❏ VISA   ❏ AMEX

Signature _____

(if paying with a credit card you must sign this form.)

Shipping and Handling charges:*

Domestic: $4 for 1st book, $.75 each additional book. International: $5 for 1st book, $1 each additional book
*rates in effect at time of publication. Subject to Change.

Mail order to Publishers Group West, Attention: Order Dept., 1700 Fourth St., Berkeley, CA 94710, or fax to (510) 528-3444.

PLEASE ALLOW 4-6 WEEKS FOR DELIVERY. ALL ORDERS SHIP VIA 4TH CLASS MAIL.

Look for Blue Moon Books at your favorite local bookseller
or from your favorite online bookseller.